Tales in the City

Volume I

Adapted into Short Film

Ukiyoto Publishing

All global publishing rights are held by

Ukiyoto Publishing

Published in 2022

Content Copyright © Ukiyoto
ISBN 9789360163808

All rights reserved.
No part of this publication may be reproduced,
transmitted, or stored in a retrieval system, in any
form by any means, electronic, mechanical,
photocopying, recording or otherwise, without the
prior permission of the publisher.

The moral rights of the author have been asserted.

This is a work of fiction. Names, characters, businesses,
places, events, locales, and incidents are either the
products of the author's imagination or used in a
fictitious manner. Any resemblance to actual persons,
living or dead, or actual events is purely coincidental.

This book is sold subject to the condition that it shall
not by way of trade or otherwise, be lent, resold, hired
out or otherwise circulated, without the publisher's
prior consent, in any form of binding or cover other
than that in which it is published.

Contents

Short Story by Riddhima Sen	1
Short Story by Chinmoy Nath	4
Short Story by Mahendra Arya	11
Short Stories by Juju's Pearls	20
Short Story by Pabitra Adhikary	43
Short Story by Ashim Basnet	47
Short Story by Revathi Raj Iyer	60
Poem by Harinder Cheema	78
Short Story by Barnali Basu	81
Short Story by Tulika Majumder	95
About the Authors	*114*

Short Story by Riddhima Sen

Bloody Snowflakes

May 2000.

The morning sun shone radiantly across the horizon. It was a warm, sunlit morning in the city of Chicago. Sam, a software engineer at a multinational company, BlueWays, was sitting on the porch of his apartment. There was a blue coffee cup on the porcelain table. An ashtray filled with burnt cigarettes lay beside the cup. It was around 10 a.m. in the morning. The lush green porch shone bright green in the dazzling sunlight, devoid of any particular hue. A book titled "A Yellow Sky " was in his hands. Sam was deeply engrossed while reading the book. It was a tale of deep, engraved sorrow. The story of an orphan teenager, who fought against the crude society to fulfill his dream of becoming a cricketer, in the snowy land of Alaska.

Sam could resonate with the poor boy's struggle for sustenance. He himself was an orphan. He aspired to become a renowned radio jockey from the age of 11. A young and loving couple had adopted him 11 years ago, from an orphanage in Chicago. They were more than his own parents to him since they showered tremendous love on him. Currently, he is one of the top radio jockeys at Blue Moon FM Studio. Although it was a part-time job, he enjoyed his work. He lived all alone, and his adoptive parents had passed away in an accident, over a year ago. When he reached the thirty-fourth page of the book, suddenly the doorbell rang. He proceeded to open the door and stared at the gigantic grandfather clock on the eastern wall. A young boy, around 11 years old, stood outside the door. He was clad in tattered clothes, and told him "Do you want to buy some snacks?" The boy seemed identical to the protagonist of the story. Even he used to sell warm snacks in the cold neighbourhood.

Sam took some burgers and paid him ten dollars. The boy left immediately. He returned to the spacious patio consequently. The bright afternoon sun shone radiantly across the red horizon, it was 1 pm the day. After devouring a sumptuous lunch comprising bacon, peas, potatoes, and warm chicken soup, he fell asleep on the couch. Abruptly, he found himself inside the story. It was Timmy, the protagonist of the story by Robert White, a renowned author. He was travelling across the snow-laden paths and crossroads when he stumbled across a mob chasing a rebel. He was hit by a bullet all of a sudden.

The next day, Sam was found dead by the police on his couch, caked with blood, and a pistol lay at his side. His blood was splattered on the snow inside a glass globe, which had broken into pieces, completely shattered into million pieces. No one knew how he passed away, despite the anti-depressant pills found in his chamber. Maybe, it was telepathy, who knows.

Short Story by Chinmoy Nath

The Centenarian Granny

Dedicated to the omnipotent source of all knowledge that manifests dreams into reality, emotions into words, and arouses liveliness in my works.

Staring and pretending to touch the hilltops from far away and touching the clouds are mere imaginations, but in real life, they are dissimilar matters of question. Building a house and maintaining relations are different things till someone takes the accountability of holding a relationship and creating a home of emotions rather than a house of bricks.

"Will you believe, if I say in our times we had a habit of clicking photos and preserving them in albums. It was far better than today's clicked images on cellphones. You click hundreds of images and delete them whenever the memory is full. In this way, you lose some precious moments. I feel very sorry for the 21st-century technical human", as Mrs. Watson was emptying her words and emotions, collecting the old photos one by one from an old worn-out album, a photograph caught her attention. Staring at the photo for some time, Mrs.Watson shouted, "Noah, who kept this photo in my album?" Mrs. Watson turned the photo upside down and looked from all angles, but couldn't identify the one in the photo. Suddenly, she shouted in amusement, "Finally I got you, Merlyn."

"Granny, she is not Marlyn. Put on your spectacles, and have a closer look. From which angle she looks like Marlyn", spoke out irritated Noah.

Though Noah confidently said that the girl in the picture was not Merlyn, he didn't know who Marlyn was. The way he objected to his grandmother's words proved that he had something to do with the girl in the picture.

"By the way how are you so confident that she is not Merlin," asked Mrs. Watson as she took out her pair of artificial teeth to clean them.

"No granny no....learn a bit of cleanliness, clean them as you used to clean your original teeth. Do you think, I'll always look after you, I have my work to do; why don't you understand," said Noah.

"Ha ha ha, you are not a girl Noah. You will be here till I die, even if you marry someone, you will not go to live in her place," the old granny couldn't stop herself from breaking into a peal of loud laughter.

Once again her pair of artificial teeth flew into the air to feel its independence. Mrs. Watson somehow managed to pick them up and adjust them in the proper place.

"Granny, look at your face, it's looking liking like a joker," Noah spoke as he held a mirror in front of her.

"Why is it so? I was more than ok a couple of minutes ago, I was more beautiful than ever, a couple of minutes ago" said the old granny as if it shouldn't have happened.

"Granny your teeth, they got jumbled, upper set fell into the lower jaw and the lower set jumped up in the upper jaw."

Noah adjusted her pair of artificial teeth in the perfect position and hugged Mrs. Watson tightly. "Granny I can't say how much I love you. I cannot let you go. If we are to forget everything why He has given us the sweet memories from which we can never part."

The old lady who has challenged death several times and crossed her centuries was put in an old age home. It was a tradition of the so-called high-class society. After Mr.Watson's death, there was nobody to look after his wife.

"Noah, let us go. Your granny will be looked after better in the old age home. She has played her innings well; it's your turn to build your career and a new home," as Noah's father packed all the belongings of Mrs. Watson, his mother, Noah protested in the middle.

" No dad, you can't do this. I can't be so modern that I can leave my dear granny to die in an unknown place, no dad no, it's not fair."

Noah once again found himself in the present when he heard his granny chuckling.

" Hello, dear what about Alzamato. I know it is eating me up. But you are with me. Where are your mom and dad? Don't you feel alone here Noah".

Noah tried to confuse her memory once again,

"Granny, do you remember who Marlyn is," though his mind whispered in his inner core, " My dear Granny, it's not Alzamato but it's Alzheimer's."

Mrs. Watson shook her head and rolled her head randomly as if she was searching for a missing link. She searched the album once again and finally took out the same photograph and once again shouted in amusement," Finally I got you, Merlyn".

" Granny, how many times I have to say, " This is not Merlyn? This is my wife, your granddaughter-in-law, Amelia. It sometimes becomes a tough job to make you understand, Granny. Do you remember Granny, I told you several times I am married. I left mom and Dad just because they transferred you to an old age home. I can't express my love, but I love you so much granny, my sweet granny." Noah kissed his sweet granny several times and broke down into tears.

" Why are you crying like a baby Noah, I know this is not Marlyn, but look at this word which is written in clear bold letters, Marlyn. Marlyn is my nickname. I thought I would forget, so wrote my nickname here on the backside of the photo."

As Mrs. Watson turned the backside of the photograph towards Noah, he saw the written name, Marlyn.

Noah broke down into loud laughter and his sweet granny joined him in his celebration.

Amelia a neuropsychiatrist, the second half of Noah never complained about her unacceptance by Noah's granny. Sometimes she was treated as a housemaid, sometimes as Noah's friend, and sometimes as Dr. Amelia. Amelia knows the condition of old age much better than Noah.

" Finally, the mystery of Marlyn is solved. Did you notice Noah, granny has preserved more than hundreds of photographs, but selected the backside of my photograph to recognize her nickname? I loved you, Noah, it's a tough decision to leave your parents to take care of your granny. But, I'll be happier if you will give me a chance to serve your parents in their old age. It's the bitter truth of life Noah. I know you see life through God's eyes and I through yours. I love you."

Amelia didn't even complete her words when Mrs. Watson started hers once again.

" Hello, once again you are here. My grandson is a very shy fellow. Why don't you both tie up in a permanent relationship; you better get married, I have heard you say that you love him."

Amelia smiled at her words which were her routine. Noah joined them in the talk and with raising brows and an act of wonder he spoke humorously.

" This girl will not leave me, granny. What to do?"

Mrs. Watson as a judge in the session court gave her final judgment.

" What to do…what to do. Your friend is so sweet, I liked her attitude. My dear Noah, you find a proper date and marry your friend as soon as possible. Permission granted."

The entire house was filled with the sounds of laughter and positive vibes.

Nobody cares about old age. When one reaches this phase, one needs company. Those who get it in their final hours are the luckiest in the entire galaxy.

Mrs. Watson got heaven on earth through his grandson and granddaughter-in-law and they through their sweet sweet granny Marlyn.

Short Story by Mahendra Arya

Twilight of life

It was extremely cold outside. Everything was snow cladded. Temperature was minus five degrees Celsius. Buffalo is colder than other towns in vicinity; perhaps due to ever flowing Niagra fall. Hotel was hardly occupied. This was not the season for the tourists.

There was a river on the back side of the hotel. The water was converted into a large ice slab.

Seventy years old Amruta pulled herself closer to the fire place. She was trying to read a novel in Hindi. Light was not sufficient for a good reading. Outside the window, it was dark even though it was day time. Lobby had the old-fashioned yellow lights. So the conditions not favourable for reading! But as she had nothing much to do, she continued her struggle with the book.

In this season it was difficult to distinguish between day and night. Day light was for few hours, rest of the time it was all dark. Not a good time indeed for general tourists, but for an introvert like Amruta this was the right place and right time. She enjoyed being in a secluded location. She enjoyed her solitude!

An old man came near her. He was limping. He looked smart in his overcoat and hat. He had a fancy white beard. He came near Amruta and asked, "If you do not mind, can I sit here near the fireplace."

Amruta gave a good look at him. He was tall and handsome. She responded, "Of course, you may please. It is so cold today."

The gentleman thanked her. He removed his overcoat and hat and hung the same on a stand provided nearby. He pulled a chair near the fireplace and sat with an angular position facing Amruta.

Amruta asked, "Are you an Indian? You look like though."

Man said, "Of course I am. I guessed that you are too; because of that hindi book in your hands. Hmm Dharmveer Bharti? What is the title?"

Amruta said, " 'Gunahon Ka Devta'"

"Can I see this?"

Amruta forwarded the book towards him and said, "Sure, please !"

He browsed the book for few pages and then came back to second page on which her name was written along with some gift message.

He said, "Story of Chandar and Sudha is so engrossing that you can read it many times. My favourite too!" He returned the book.

"So your name is Amruta Gujral; where do you belong to?"

She replied, "I come from a town called Rohtak in Haryana. Where are you from?"

He fumbled a bit, then said, "Actually now I belong to this place only, as I have been here for a very long time. In fact I am the manager of this hotel."

"Very nice place this is. How long have you been here?"

"More than fifty years now."

Amruta laughed and said, "Oh, then you are almost an American now! Where does your family live?"

"No one to call a family! Lost my father in childhood. Mother was with me but she expired about twelve years ago. No siblings! Unmarried!

What about your family, Amruta ji?"

"I did not marry; hence I will be single forever. I enjoy reading and writing, so life is pivoted around this hobby."

"That is strange! In Indian society girls cannot stay unmarried; in fact.

The parents insist on getting their daughter married. Then why…, I am sorry, these are your personal matters. Don't tell if you are not comfortable."

Amruta said with a melancholy smile, "At this point in life, there is nothing which needs to be personal. A writer like me is like an open book. I do write my life only in my stories. I did not marry, just like that."

Man asked, "You did not find anyone worthy of you? But that seems unlikely. I read on the second page of your book – Presented to Dear Amruta with lots of sweet memories! Signed by Pancham Ralhan! Why, what happened to Mr. Ralhan?"

Amruta blushed on being caught and exposed about her past by a stranger. Finally decided to tell the facts.

"Nothing very serious about him. My parents decided to find a match for me when I was young , maybe in my early twenties. They found this gentleman Pancham Ralhan. He visited Rohtak and stayed for a week.

My parents encouraged me to meet him regularly to make up my mind. That gave some time to Pancham to decide about me. It was a good time of my life. During that courtship, he presented this book to me. To tell you the truth, I had started liking him."

Man smiled and said, "See how I got the truth out of you. But you have not completed the story. You started liking him, then what went wrong? Did he not approve of you? Why did you not marry him?

Sorry once again, I am entering into your personal life. Please share only if you wish to."

Amruta gave a smile. Then said, "You must be anticipating some great failed love story, like Chander and Sudha? But it is not so. Knowing my feelings, my parents gave him our consent. Pancham was working somewhere abroad, he promised to come back with his family within a month for the marriage. He personally promised to take me along after the marriage. That is where my love story ended. He never came back. Nor did he write any letter. Maybe he changed his mind. I was optimistic in my heart; but that optimism also was over, when my father informed me that he had formally written 'A No' for this arrangement. Though as such it was not difficult for me to forget everything; however that experience left a scar on my heart. Why do people behave in a certain way by giving all kinds of commitments and then change so much that they don't even try to communicate again."

He could see a sadness in the eyes of Amruta; a moist layer was visible in her eyes. He said, "He did an injustice to you. Such an attitude is certainly condemnable."

Amruta realized that she was enjoying this conversation with this stranger. She decided to probe into his life.

"Hey, you got my past out from me. Now you too owe the same to me. Why did you not marry ever?"

He laughed out heartily. Then said, "My story is even more hopeless than yours. The Indians living in America prefer to get girls from India only. So they visit India. Their relatives, friends or even matrimonial agents arrange the match making. So one has to make his selection out of such meetings."

Amruta said jokingly, "So you could not find anyone suitable for yourself?"

Gentleman laughed, "No no ! It is not that bad a love story. I found one. I presumed she also liked me. We fixed a date for the wedding within a couple of months. But as you know, man proposes God disposes. I met with a road accident. My left foot got crushed; hence it had to be amputated. The limp in my walk is because of the artificial foot fixed with the stump of my amputated foot."

Amruta expressed with sorrow, "That is very sad. So the girl refused to marry you with your amputated foot."

"I do not know. I had no courage to contact the girl. I wrote to her father about the developments with me. I gave him an option to break the commitment as no father would like to get his daughter married to a handicapped person. I expected a letter of rejection from the girl's father, though I thought that the girl might be considerate as we had shared a good wave length."

Amruta said, "It must have been tough on the girl. Girls are very soft hearted. Once they start liking someone, it is difficult for them to say no. But if she said so, I do not have any complaints against her. You should also not remember her with any negativity in your heart."

"Of course, never! I never felt any negativity towards her. The reply from the father was on the expected lines; but a communication from her would have served like a balm on my wounds. Just like your own feelings, Amruta!"

Amruta felt better after he shared the hidden pains of his heart. She also liked when he dropped the respectful suffix of 'Ji' after her name.

"We all carry some pains or wounds within ourselves; for whatever reasons we never want to discuss those with anyone. But today I feel really good having shared mutual life and experiences."

He started getting up. He said, "Indeed, I too feel better after talking to you. We all are lonely. A company of a few hours is also a comfort for us. It was a pleasure talking to you Amruta ! If you wish, you may have dinner with me."

"Why not? In fact dinner was not on the cards for me tonight, but I cannot refuse a dinner with your company."

He wore his overcoat and hat. He said, "In that case we meet in the restaurant at seven o clock."

He started going away.

Amruta called him, "Hey listen !"

He turned back.

She said,"How stupid of me! We talked for such a long time. I even accepted your invitation for dinner; but I did not ask your name."

He stood there with a long endearing smile. And said – "I am Pancham Ralhan !"

Amruta looked at him mesmerized for a while. She felt that they resumed where they had left in Rohtak forty five years ago.

Short Stories by Juju's Pearls

Casual relationship!

Prelude

Modernization is constant and is a challenging word. Eastern world is adopting western culture and western world is adopting eastern culture. As Earth is rotating and revolving, a paradigm shift has been observed in the values and ethics of the human race. We will deal with the concept of marriage, which of late has been redefined. In an era of women empowerment and modernization, there is a palpable fear of commitment amongst the new generation. Many have adopted the western idea of live-in relationship or Casual relationship.

In the latter there is bonding without love. The main ingredient of love is missing. Such relationships are with mutual consent and do not require emotional involvement. Primal physical needs are satisfied and have a low maintenance cost.

This is one such modern story about Sugandha and Vijay.

Sugandha was a well-educated, independent, happy girl who lived in a metro city. She had a normal healthy upbringing. In her household, her parents treated her and her brother in the same manner. Being the elder, she always had a say in family discussions. She had big brown eyes and long hair till her mid-thigh. Her walk oozed confidence and happiness. She worked for a big corporate company in her city.

Once, while going to the temple, she was hit by a car. She almost missed hitting her head on the ground by extending her both palms. The fall of impact was borne by her both wrist joints. She feared she had fractured her right wrist bones. The pain was unbearable and she started crying. In this whole chaos, she did not hear the car screeching to halt, soon after it hit her. Suddenly she felt a man's hand on her shoulder. Wiping her tears, she saw an elderly gentleman with the most generous smile. He politely asked her, "Child, you were walking on the wrong side, I am sorry for this. Let me take you to the hospital." With onlookers help, Sugandha sat in the car and rode with him. Luckily, she had minor bruises and was discharged after dressings. The elderly gentleman offered to pay the bills and told his driver to drop Sugandha at her home.

She was impressed by the fine mannerisms of the elderly gentleman. After a few days, her wounds healed. She went to the temple to seek blessings from God before resuming her work. As she was climbing the steps, she saw the elderly gentleman with a woman and a young man. Sugandha turned and started walking in the opposite direction. After a few meters, she found herself face to face with the man. The man recognized her and introduced his wife and son to her. Greeting exchanged, he invited her for a cup of tea at his house. All this while, his son seemed least interested in talking to her. Sugandha assumed him to be arrogant.

Accepting the tea invite Sugandha went to the gentleman's house. It was obvious that the couple was awestruck with her. She felt uncomfortable and thought of leaving early. The elderly woman spoke, 'Dear, I am so sorry for making you uncomfortable. You are the kind of girl we are looking for our son, Vijay. He is not interested in getting married. In case you like us and Vijay, we will like to come with our proposal to your house." Sugandha knew this was coming. She had checked on Vijay and his pleasant personality had appealed to her. She gave a benefit of doubt for his arrogance too and thought it was a good sign when boys didn't talk much with girls. His features were on his father. The couple went and spoke to Vijay. Through the glass door, Sugandha could not make out what they were talking about. But the body language of their son clearly conveyed that he was not interested. She left without saying anything.

This meeting was buried in her mind and life went on as usual. Sugandha's mother noticed a change in her behaviour and when confronted, she blamed it on stress at work. All this while, she could not forget Vijay's face. Deep inside, she knew he was the one for him. The pressure from her parents to get married started mounting up. She thought of going to the temple with the hope of meeting Vijay's parents. It seemed the universe had conspired for their meet. Sugandha climbed up the steps and walked straight inside to offer flowers. She closed her eyes and started praying. Suddenly, a voice spoke in her ears,' Are you praying for us?" She saw Vijay standing next to her, his elbow touching her elbow and he winked, "Am I am right or am I not wrong?" His sense of humour broke the ice and she smiled. He further continued, "If you are done with your prayers, let's talk over tea at the nearby café. I remember you left your tea last time."

At the café, Vijay spoke first. He said, "I apologize for my parent's straight forward question. They like you very much and want you to see you as my life partner. Even I find you very beautiful and appealing and would love to have a relationship with you. But! he paused. Sugandha patiently waited for him to complete the sentence in order to understand what was going on in his mind. After sipping the entire tea, he took a deep sigh and continued, "Please don't judge me. I am very clear about certain things in my life. I don't believe in getting married. We are mature adults and can opt for a relationship without giving it a name. Hope you understand."

Sugandha was confused and did not know where the talk was heading. The key words kept popping up in her mind, relationship without a name, what was the need to enter such a relationship and what was the flipside. As if reading her state of mind, Vijay continued, "Let me complete. Look, I had a disturbed childhood. I have witnessed my parent's arguments and fights. They always fought like enemies when they were young and I was a child. Now they have matured and live like a made for each other couple. They don't realize I have scars from my childhood. I was sent to a boarding school for the same reason. Surprisingly, they think they don't have a witness to their fights during the initial decade of their married life."

Sugandha smiled for the very first time since they had met. Vijay seemed to relax and assumed they were in the same level of thoughts. And he continued, "So, are you okay with us being in a Casual relationship?" This last line was like a whip lashing statement and Sugandha spoke, "Casual! What do you mean?" Now, it was Vijay's turn for the confused expression, "I thought you understood where my talk was heading to! Didn't you? Why did you smile then?"

Sugandha broke into laughter and replied in between gasping for air and her laugh, "I assumed your talk was heading towards the disclosure of the fact that you are gay, but it was the other way round. Now this term, Casual relationship is new to me. And I am not interested in even knowing about it. I am a simple girl. This term doesn't go where there are prospects of marriage. Now, may I take your leave?" Sugandha rose from her chair and was about to leave when Vijay reached out to her and pulled her towards him.

The touch was electrifying and she felt unknown sensations run down her spine and her head started to spin. She sat down and drank water. Vijay requested her to give him a chance to explain himself. He elaborated further, "Casual relationship is the new trend. Why commit when you can enjoy everything without the label of marriage? Emotions are not involved and there is a free exit. Doesn't it sound convenient?"

Sugandha banged her glass on the table and said," No! I don't see it like this. Marriage is not for convenience and there is no term like free exit. It's about two people who decide to spend their lives together and have families. I am a one-man woman, who values her morals and ethics. As for me, I need to be emotionally involved before getting physical and if there is no emotional involvement, how can one come close and have a physical relationship. I beg to differ and genuinely I appreciate your openness. There is nothing unethical or immoral about it, I want to stand corrected. Let's leave it on this note."

Vijay fell short of words and didn't know what to reply. He just looked up in the air with palm facing upwards. "Hey, I thought you were an educated, open minded modern girl, but you sound conservative and old fashioned."

These words were the threshold limit for Sugandha. She leaned forwards and placed her palms on the table and in a most calm voice said, "Look Vijay, don't bring these terms of conservative, old fashioned, modern girl etc. I know what you are trying to convey. But unfortunately, you don't understand what I am trying to convey. Being open minded and modern doesn't imply that one wears revealing clothes or takes hard drinks as men do. A man's lifestyle is not a benchmark for women, at least for me. I am educated, open minded with a purpose in my life. This doesn't make me conservative or old fashioned. The main difference between mankind and other species is being responsible, civilized and committed. These are virtues which require immense will power and only a strong-minded person can afford these virtues."

Vijay's jaw dropped as he looked at her while she spoke. She raised her right hand to signal him not to interrupt her. She continued, "If anyone starts any journey with a negative thought then the whole purpose is defeated. How can you talk about free exit while being in a relationship? This sounds contradictory. One cannot succeed if one keeps thinking about failures. The mindset is totally different in both scenarios. So, my dear Vijay, just because I dress simply, don't take alcohol or wear short dresses doesn't make me any less. And your opinion, who even cares? Think about it. Grow up. Be a man and take charge of at least your own life. You are drifting and so are your friends. Life is way beyond what you have shared. I prefer to be in my conscious state and enjoy each moment rather than be in an intoxicated state. Every life has a purpose. Identify yours."

With this, Sugandha picked up her bag. Vijay's expressions were as if he had been struck by lightning. His lips curved into a smile and he said, "Now I know why my parents want you to be my life partner. They are not happy with my life choices and friend circle." Sugandha sat down and said, "Let's do the closure. We have met for a purpose. I am an educated, independent girl who makes her own decisions. This is my definition of being modern, open minded. Our values and purpose are different. I wish you luck." She got up and flashed her beautiful smile and paid half the bill amount. She winked and said," You just lost one of the most amazing persons on this planet as your life partner."

After this, they never even attempted to stay in touch. Few years later, they again met in the temple. Sugandha was with her spouse and two children. Vijay looked haggard as he had been in a series of casual relationships. Their eyes met, acknowledged and they walked in different directions. Every human being has to take charge of his life and make decisions in a conscious state. It takes immense strength to tread on the righteous path. Being in a conscious, committed state is the highest level of intoxication. Get addicted to this.

Journey of Gopi

Prelude

Life is all about making choices. Many souls come and many go. Once in many centuries a soul takes birth which tries to challenge the age-old traditions, and lives life on his terms. This one such story of a boy called Gopi who was born into an affluent family. He challenged his family tradition and was literally locked horns with his mother. There were many daring choices he made and always took the onus on himself.

This story will take the readers through his life span of eight decades, about his choices, his success, his failures and regrets if any. A tribute to his bravery, courage to weather the storms and get his life ship sailed smoothly in the unpredicted Ocean of life and anchor safely. Gopi is truly an ordinary soul who lived an extraordinary life and left a huge legacy of wisdom, morals, ethics besides monetary.

The scene is set in a semi-rural region of the oldest country on this Mother Earth. A fair, handsome boy is born in a rich affluent family. As he takes color after his father, he looks like a faded version of his elder brother who has a dark complexion owing to their mother's genes. The first son is an obedient child who knows the ways of the world and how to impress parents and other subjects with sugar coated talks. Second son is our main hero around whom our story is woven. Being a naughty child, his parents name him Gopi after Hindu God Krishna who is an epitome of mischievousness in his childhood stories.

Gopi had an independent mindset and thinking of his own. His elder brother had not enrolled in school as per their parent's wishes. The sole idea was family business. As a child he questioned his mother's age old traditions and always asked for logic behind. He was shunned and scolded by his mother for being inquisitive. As he turned three, he urged his father to get him enrolled in school. His father was a broad thinker. He never discouraged even though he never encouraged either.

School admission was a source of immense joy for Gopi. He felt he had stepped into an entirely different world. He was very good in academics and extracurricular activities. During harvesting season, he developed an eye infection. His parents consulted a local doctor and appropriate medicine was advised. Till date, he is unable to figure out what went wrong that ill fated night. His mother had put eye drops as advised by the doctor and patched his affected eye. The next morning, his vision had diminished. This was my first blow as a primary school child. Reasons were two, either the dose of medication was more than recommended or the patch had been kept for an unusually longer time. This incident left a deep scar in the child's heart and mind.

During his middle school years, he happened to overhear a conversation between his parents which took the ground below his feet. As they were five siblings, his father was considering giving his second son for adoption to his younger brother who was childless. He pledged he will not be adopted. One of his school friend's had been given for adoption in his family relations and had a bad experience. After hearing his story, Gopi told his parents straightforwardly to consider someone else for this purpose. This decision and confrontation transformed him. That day he learnt he had to learn to speak for himself and be in a position to defend him.

Gradually he withdrew from his favourite sports and immersed himself in books. He did his master's and went abroad for higher studies. This was another feather in his rebellious cap. As if going to school was not enough, he did his masters and went for doctorate. Going against his mother's wishes he married an educated girl was the biggest feather in his rebellious cap. By this time, he had been labelled as a rebel.

He started his marital life in a metro city and took up a job in a reputed firm. Life was beautiful and they started enjoying the journey. Soon, stork visited them and this good news acted like an ice breaker between him and his parents. To make things right, Gopi and his wife decided to go for delivery in their hometown.

His wife cautioned him about the lack of medical facilities there. Gopi took this news as a sign from God to create peace with his parents. God had different plans.

Just before his due date, Gopi had to rush to the city for some urgent work. His wife requested him to let her accompany him, which he politely refused after counselling her that it was a one day trip. This ill fated day is the second biggest regret in Gopi's life. No sooner had he left, his wife went into labour and delivered a baby boy who was in distress. As there was no immediate medical intervention, the baby could not announce his arrival. This day became the darkest day in Gopi's life as he felt guilty about leaving his wife behind in spite of her requests.

Life goes on and one tends to learn to live with all grief and sadness. Few years later, his wife conceived again and they were blessed with a handsome baby. This acted like a balm and they started living happily. Gopi was earning well and his life seemed balanced and he was blessed with a beautiful daughter. Their family frame seemed perfect. Life gives blows off and on and Gopi braves them with his loving wife by his side. He had few changes of jobs which led to interval stretches of uncertainty. Gopi had gradually learnt to play his cards well. Whenever there was a period of unemployment, his rental income kept the household functioning and all his expenses were met.

The next challenge to overcome was the marriage of his children. He had saved wisely and was able to keep his ship afloat in these challenging times. All this while, he had unconditional support of his loving, caring, independent wife. She was his main driving force and epicentre of recharge. With her by his side he felt invincible, unstoppable.

After every few months, life changes colour and throws in stones. His daughter started facing domestic violence, abuse. She was forced by her in-laws to leave her child. She came back to her parent's house. Gopi had never imagined he would spend his retirement period going round the district courts. All his hard work got the judgement in their favour. Gopi's daughter got custody of her child. On his wife's suggestion, he bought a flat in her name and ensured she had a source of income. Being educated, his daughter got a job as per her profile.

Soon after, Gopi's son suffered a massive loss in his business. To save his son from going into depression, Gopi broke his fixed deposits in banks and his provident fund. He was wise enough to keep his wife's account safe.

He and his wife had just stabilized from the double trauma of their children, when his wife started having heart problems. His assets were empty by now. Hiding from his wife, he applied for a bank loan to take care of medical expenditure. Gopi was not aware that his intelligent wife had already made a will in his name. With finances being taken care of, he got the best treatment for his wife. Things started improving and flowers were blossoming back in their lives.

Gopi's wife left her mortal coil in her sleep. Gopi was oblivious that on ill fated night, his wife had crossed to another dimension. She was his backbone and had always been a pillar of support. This was the final blow. Gopi felt weak and wanted to join her. His children gave him the much needed emotional support and tried to be his clutches. Gopi's heart bled as he yearned for his soul mate's company.

One day, he silently prayed to God, "Oh God, living without her is like a torture, please help me in joining her." That night, his wife came into his dreams, they chatted. Gopi enjoyed and lived every moment. Before bidding him bye, she turned back and smiled, "Gopi, I love you and I know you love me more. Believe me, I am fine and happy. Your time is not now. You have to take care of our children. They need you more than me. When the right time comes, I will come to take you with me. Take care of your health for our children's sake."

Next morning brought new hope and enthusiasm in Gopi's life. Now he was content and satisfied. All his regrets seemed to have evaporated. He focussed on positive aspects and gradually his health improved. At times, when he is alone, he ponders about these magical nights. Now he knows a way to reach out to his beloved. This mere thought gives him solace and push to go on. Each night he prays to God and waits for his wife. He knows when the right time comes, his wife will be there waiting for him.

Victim of Gaslighting?

Prelude

Gas lighting as the name suggests is not related to actual objects in our kitchens. This is a recent term used to address mental games played by individuals in an endeavour to demean and suppress the weaker one and establish one's own supremacy. The actions are such that they are seldom obvious to the third person. This phenomenon is experienced by the doer and the victim.

The actions are subtle and targeted with the aim to disturb and destroy the victim's mental peace. This story revolves around Urmilla, her challenges and her victory.

Urmilla was a girl from a low socio-economic strata and a simple, humble background. Her father was a peon in a government post office. And her mother used to do household chores in neighbouring apartments. To give Urmilla a better life, her parents encouraged and motivated her to study and become financially independent. She was adorable, sincere and hardworking. She was well aware that her parents were working hard to make ends meet. In spite of meagre resources, they treated her like a princess.

High school life had various challenges. Monica was the daughter of the trustee of their school. She liked to be called by her pet name 'Maddy'. She behaved as if she owned the school and always bullied other girls. Urmilla was very good in academics and debates. She was a teacher and everyone's favourite. This irked Maddy as she considered herself to be the Best. How could a poor girl steal limelight from her?

Soon the School Captain elections were announced. Maddy was sure of her win and didn't even bother to campaign. Other girls had pitched Urmilla against her. On the day of results, everyone was in a state of shock as Urmilla won with a clean sweep. This was too much for Maddy to bear. She created her wretched plan to break Urmilla's confidence and self esteem.

On the day of the Oath ceremony, she smeared Urmilla's skirt with a magic color which turned red when in contact with water. Unaware of Maddy's plan, Urmilla sat on the chair as directed. She was not aware the chair was wet. When she got up for her speech and turned around, there was a big gasp amongst everyone. Her dress had a big red patch. Soon there were giggles and hustled voices. Urmilla gave a confused expression and was about to hold the mike for her welcome address, when the Principal came with a big shawl, wrapped it around her and sent her to the Recovery room. On her way she saw red drops on the floor and immediately understood the reason for everyone's reaction. She had no idea what was going on.

Principal and staff held an inquiry committee to probe this incident. But no evidence could be gathered against anyone. This matter was closed and Maddy celebrated her own victory. Whenever she was with Urmilla, she would behave in a way to make herself appear superior and speak demeaning words with her group targeting her. The cafe incident opened Urmilla's eyes. Once in the Cafe Maddy tried to trip on Urmillla and spilled her tea on her dress. Instead of saying Sorry, she started abusing Urmilla for standing in her way and not moving out of the way, rather accusing her as the reason for her fall and her tea. Urmilla apologized and left.

Urmilla's friend who was a witness realized what was happening. She told her about Maddy playing mind games. Superficially, she appeared to be a caring friend of Urmilla and internally she was hatching plans to demean her.

School lessons are seldom forgotten. In college life, Urmilla found her at the receiving end once again. When she topped her university exam, her roommate and ace competitor, Sonia floated the false news about her doing favours for the external examiner. Back in the hostel, Sonia was the first one to console Urmilla and pledged to find out about this rumour. But the cat had been let out of the bag and the reputation had been tarnished.

All this while Urmilla kept blaming herself and started working on herself to avoid such untoward incidents. She finished college. One day she was going home with her father after submitting documents for her Master's degree. At the roundabout, an over speeding car came and hit her father from behind. She saw her father's body being lifted in the air, flipped twice and fell on the road. As the head hit the concrete road, the skull fractured and there was a pool of blood. Her father died on the spot. She pledged to catch the culprit and get him punished.

Onlookers had noted the car number. With great help from police she traced the culprit and filed a charge sheet against him. It turned out that the driver was a teenage boy of the Minister's politician standing in the upcoming elections.

To save his reputation, the Minister politician approached Urmilla's mother and offered hefty compensation. Her mother was more concerned about her daughter's marriage. The chair addiction in politics is really bad. The Minister offered the alliance of his elder son with Urmilla if the case was withdrawn.

Urmilla was against this proposal but her mother pressured her to agree to the proposal. Soon, the engagement ceremony was done in a low key affair. Urmilla withdrew the case. The marriage was solemnized in a local temple. Urmilla later realized that she had been married to the bodyguard of Minister's elder son who himself was a loyal slave to the minister. After the wedding her now husband ordered her not to change the wedding dress and wait for her master to return.

She waited patiently till way beyond half past midnight. She started pondering about being at the receiving end. She knew her low socio economic status was the main reason. Even though she was beautiful and excelled in studies, her status overshadowed everything. She made a resolve to take charge of her life from that moment. Suddenly, she felt the room door open and shut and someone came and lay beside her. She assumed that person to be her husband. When she turned around, she saw the Minister's son smiling at her with his tongue rolling against his cheek. She knew she was trapped and her modesty was at stake. Suddenly, she felt a man's hand on her shoulder from her end of the bed. On seeing her husband she immediately got up and stood behind him. Her husband pulled her from behind and threw her on the bed in front of her master. He bowed and said, "I am my master's slave and whatever is mine will be my master's." On hearing this, Urmilla knew the only way to get out of this situation was to feign unconsciousness. This irked the master and he left angrily.

Next day, on the pretext of going to her mother's place she took a train to a far away state. She called her mother there too. She briefed her mother about the deceit. She decided to pursue her studies and her mother supported her financially by doing household chores. She worked hard to give wings to her parent's dream. She cracked the civil services examinations in first attempt. She returned to her hometown as the District Collector. She had changed her name from Urmilla to Monica.

After living a challenging life since childhood, she returned as Monica to slay all her opponents in a similar way. It was payback time and none was spared.

Urmilla's father often smiles from up amongst clouds and blesses his naive daughter for transforming into an amazing person with a dangerously level of confidence. The culprits will be punished and judgement day was in sight now.

Be a Womb Protector - Save the Girl Child

Women are the highest evolved species. And they are God's favourite too. As God entrusted the most important thing "Womb" in woman. Womb is the place where creation and nurturing goes hand in hand.

With these lines, I rest my case and request all discussions about weaker sex, fairer sex, women empowerment etc to cease. Women are already empowered by God. The only thing is, either they have forgotten this or have been made believe this. Suits men!

Time to remind ourselves

No girl child, no sister to tie rakhi,

No girl child, no kanjakaan for pooja

No girl child, no bride

No girl child, no house, only concrete home

No girl child, no laughter

No girl child, no magic.

No girl child, no beauty

Soon this Earth will go back to the Ice Age days. It's a wake-up call to save the girl child.

Let's pledge not interfere in God's work, accept his decisions and trust him in full faith and spirits.

It's NOW or NEVER!

Author's note: The author has tried to sensitize the readers, current challenges which we are facing in 21st century via Vijay, Sugandha, Gopi, Urmilla, Monica and Sonia

Keep loving , Keep caring

Keep reading, Keep sharing

"Helping others heal, is a path to self healing" – Juju's Pearls

Short Story by Pabitra Adhikary

An Unbelievable Love Story

I am Aniruddha Bagchi. I am one of the renowned doctors in the city of Kolkata. I am a cardiologist and 35 years old.

However, I would like to describe the incident in brief.

I saw a girl lying sick on the street. There was a minor accident between a scooty and another bike. But the girl lost consciousness.

I can't bypass a patient lying unconscious on the street in this way.

As a doctor I have a duty. I instructed my driver to assist and then I took the girl to my nursing home.

The name of that girl was Sayantini Kundu. She has come from the USA just for a year. Her age is around 30. It is ten years ago from today. Then the girl's heart was transplanted.

The donor too was a girl. Her brain died owing to an accident. Her heart was transplanted into the body of this girl. The entire process was done in the USA.

But there are a few complications in Sayantini after the heart transplantation. For example, she becomes absent-minded on the street, and even sometimes loses her consciousness etc. Many times she remembers ample memories of that old girl.

This has never been heard of in medical science.

I want to make Sayantini completely cured. But she surprised me one day when she proposed to me. Maybe she liked me.

When a girl helplessly prays for love, it feels very bad to give her back.

But it is quite impossible for me to love her. For this, one needs to hear the story of my past life.

I was born in a small village. I was proficient in studies and good at games and sports in the school of my native village.

In that village there came several families from Kolkata during the marriage of the Chowdhury house. There I was acquainted with a girl and then we became friends. Her name was Madhurima. I started loving her at the very first sight.

I have fixed in my mind that I would marry her in the future.

Madhurima also liked me but first of all I have to be worthy of her. So I started studying with great concentration. I ranked very well in the medical entrance exam. I got admitted to Kolkata Medical College.

Coming to kolkata I came to know that Madhurima's father was transferred to the USA. I talked to her over the telephone. She was glad to hear of my success.

Then came that cursed day. On that very day, I came to know the news of Madhurima's accident.

Madhurima died in a fatal accident. Her father tried hard to save her life in a large nursing home in the USA. Though her father had spent a lot of money there, she was not successful in saving the life of Madhurima.

On that day I decided in my mind to live forever in this way, cherishing her memory.

I told Sayantini everything openly.

She listened to me with rapt attention.

Then she said, "Maybe you Don't believe me. Such a memory floats before my eyes again and again. The kind of story you told, that type of picturesque village, a lad. There is a great affinity between your description and my memory."

I could not believe her words. I called that hospital in the USA where Sayantini's heart was transplanted. I wanted to know from them the name of the donor.

The answer came, "Madhurima Sanyal."

Short Story by Ashim Basnet

The Momos

The winter air was crisp and cold. Children blew hot steam from their mouths, simulating smoking. People basked in the warmth of the sun, soaking in the heat that seemed to defrost their frozen bodies, layer by layer. The sky was clear, as clear as it gets in the winter. Time seemed to drag along slowly, mesmerized by the beauty of the mountains around.

Hari was in a hurry, as always. He had been working in the small restaurant since he was eight. It was not a restaurant per se; it was more of a Deli selling Momos. It had been five years since his uncle had brought him here. His uncle had gone back to the village and left him here to survive on his own. His father had been killed by a bear in the jungle and his mother... he had no memories of her. People said that she had died while giving birth to him. Now he had no one left except his uncle—Kaka. It had been maybe three years since he last saw his old Kaka. He had nowhere to go, but life was not so bad.

It was already six in the morning, and the customers would be here in the next hour. Their restaurant served the best momos, and Hari was the specialist.

"Where have you been, you idiot? Who is going to knead the dough... your grandfather?" shouted Tashi the proprietor.

"The meat shop just opened, it seems the meat came in late, so I had to wait," Hari replied meekly. He immediately started the kneading, filled the steamer with water, and set it on the gas burner.

Generally, Tashi was good to him, apart from the occasional berating he gave during the rush hours when he lost his cool. Hari had a roof over his head and belly full of food with money to spare. What else does a man need? He had been collecting money since the day Tashi paid him his first salary and until date had amassed a wealth of about ten thousand rupees.

Whenever he was free, he would take out the bundle and count aloud for Tashi and the other helper to hear. On many occasions, his boss had rounded off the amount by filling in the gaping deficit by an extra ten or twenty. Tashi was a decent person and was good to him, good enough to be precise.

The other helper Suk was from around the area but was not a full-time employee. He would come early in the morning and leave in the afternoon, leaving the whole burden to Hari for the night, but he did help them tide over the peak hours. The cold drove most of the customers home early, and by six there would only be one or two occasional visitors. They closed by seven anyway.

The restaurant itself was Hari's residence, and at night after downing the shutters, he would have the whole setting to himself. He was the boss then. He could do whatever he wanted, and in a way, it was his home even if it was only during the night hours.

Tashi lived nearby in a small house with his wife Dicki. The couple had no children even after a decade of marriage. Sometimes they would invite Hari to their kitchen. Other times they made him cook whenever the occasion demanded, be it a party or any other function. Tashi would compensate him, and it supplemented his growing savings. Boarding and lodging being in the house, Hari hardly had any expenses.

Tashi entrusted him to the kitchen with little interference. Suk had resigned himself to being a helper second to Hari, reluctantly at first but gradually accepting his fate. He had been a helper when Hari had walked into the kitchen as a boy of eight. Hari was a hard worker and as years passed, he slowly won over his employer's confidence. It had ultimately resulted in Tashi appointing him the master of the kitchen.

"Hari, are the momos ready yet? The customer at table two has been waiting for almost half an hour," Tashi shouted over the counter, his voice carrying over to the kitchen through the steamy air.

"Just five more minutes," shouted back Hari, speeding up his movements and issuing instructions to Suk who had to double up as a waiter. Tashi entered the kitchen, indicating the rush hour. During the rush hours, Tashi usually pitched in, trying to relieve some tension from the kitchen. By about three in the afternoon, they were free to take a breather before again enacting the same routine for the evening.

Tuesday was a day off in his part of the town and Hari had the freedom to indulge in whatever he pleased. He mostly enjoyed rising late. He ate lunch and caught a movie or strolled around the main market, just enjoying his day of freedom. He also met some people, who, like himself, worked in the different restaurants and had a day off too. Over a cup of tea, the conversation usually centred on their employer or their respective salaries. Many people would recognize him, and he would be desperately trying to place them. Plenty of customers visited the restaurant, and Hari's momos were gaining popularity every day.

One Tuesday, as he loitered around the market, a man called out his name. The man was tall and fat, making him look over bearing. Hari didn't recognize him. "Hey boy... come here," the man shouted, waving his hand. Hari walked towards him, looking behind to make sure that it was him who was being beckoned.

"You... the momo boy," the man confirmed his invitation.

"Yes, sir," Hari said, unsure of what the man wanted from him.

"I love your Momos," the man said. "You have the touch, a gift. Come, let's have lunch. It's my treat." The man put an arm around Hari's shoulder. Hari was delighted to be invited to lunch by a fan of his cooking. It felt good. The man led him to a small restaurant that looked posh compared to the one he worked in.

"How long have you been working for Tashi?" the man said, indicating his acquaintance with his employer.

"Five years... Nearly six," Hari replied over a plate of rice and chicken curry.

"So, are you happy?" the man asked.

"Yeah... Tashi sir is very good to me," Hari replied, wondering where this conversation was heading.

"Have some more chicken," the man said, putting some more chicken on Hari's plate. "So, how much do you get paid?" the man asked, trying to sound as casual as possible.

"Enough..." Hari said, putting a hand on his plate.

"What?" the man asked, surprised.

"Enough chicken... I am full," Hari replied, trying to avoid the question.

For some time, the two concentrated on their plate. The conversation somewhat stalled until the man looked up and said, "If ever you want to leave Tashi, come to work for me. I will double whatever he is paying you. Maybe even give you a partnership.

Imagine owning a part of the restaurant—it is a chance of a lifetime. Think about it."

The man paid for the food and walked away, leaving a confused Hari standing alone. He stood for some time, shook his head as if to dislodge a bad thought from his mind, and continued his window-shopping. He had planned to watch a movie but it was too late now. So he just loitered around the market area before he concluded his outing and headed towards his abode. Although the road was downhill, making his journey back somewhat easier, he was tired and the thought of work the next day, dampened his spirits.

***

Life went on in a cycle, round and round, the tracks leaving behind sagging skins and receding hairlines. It had been twenty years since Hari entered the employment of Tashi. Hari had aged beyond his years, and making momos was just a reflex to him now as is breathing. In... out... in... out. Hari's momos were in great demand now, and the orders he received were beyond any human's capabilities. Suk was dead, mercifully released from life and momos. Hari had four helpers now, and the restaurant had almost tripled in size. Tashi had gone quite old and hardly came to the restaurant. It was all Hari's show, except that the money went to fill Tashi's coffers. After his wife's death, Tashi seemed to have stopped taking any burden except occasionally coming to the restaurant to show proof of his existence and ownership.

Now and then Hari still remembered the offer the man had given him. He wondered why he had not given it a second thought. Maybe he was scared then to go out of his comfort zone, or maybe he had not believed the man. He had surely missed a chance given by destiny. Now it was too late, and he would always be a slave to Tashi. Hari often regretted the decision taken a long time ago. He sometimes cursed himself, cursed his lack of courage to grab the chance of a lifetime. He could have had his own restaurant by now, could be working for himself and not for someone else... someone, who did not even care.

"Shit…" Hari shook his head, trying to dislodge the regret welling up in his head. He was sick of the same, monotonous life. He missed his home. He did not even know if he had any relatives living. Surely the old Kaka was dead. Could his children be there? "What have I to show for all the bloody hard work I put in all these years? Not even someone to call my own," Hari said to no one in particular. Biren, one of the helpers, looked at Hari and then continued to knead the dough.

"Hari… Hari… where the hell are you?" Tashi shouted over the din in the restaurant. Hari came out of the kitchen, surprised to see his boss after a long time. "*Agya*, what is wrong? Why are you here? I would have come to the house," Hari said in a hurry, calling Tashi *Agya*, a gesture of respect in the Tibetan community.

"Come to the house at night. I have called some people over to play cards. Cook something nice for us," Tashi said before turning around and walking off.

***

Four friends sat cross-legged in a circle on the carpet. Three decks of cards were mixed and twenty-one each distributed—they were playing marriage, a card game. The house looked dirty with cobwebs strategically placed all around. The cleanliness seemed to have died with Dicki. Dicki the barren, she could not give Tashi his heir, the prince for the momos… left him with only Hari.

"*Agya*, the dinner is ready," Hari announced, looking at the clock on the wall where both its hands pointed upwards indicating midnight. "Shut the hell up… and get us a bottle," Tashi slurred, staring at Hari with bloodshot eyes.

"But… but it is late, and I got to start early tomorrow," Hari rebutted softly.

"To hell with you and your momos… get me a fucking bottle. Here, take these keys and bring some money from inside," Tashi said, handing over a set of keys.

"But Agya, you get it yourself. I don't want to have anything to do with money. Dicki madam always told me not to enter the bedroom," Hari said, reluctantly taking the keys.

"Just shut up and do what I tell you, you shit. I am the boss of the house now."

Hari slowly opened the door to the bedroom, removed his shoes, and stepped inside. It felt like entering Dicki's sanctuary, his feet guiltily sliding across the wooden floor. His eyes adjusted to the dim light reflecting from a *diya*, the light flickering now and then. His eyes searched for the safe and finally stopped at one corner where the safe was sitting. He turned the keys and opened the door to the safe.

There were stacks of notes haphazardly stuffed inside and jewellery glistering against the flickering lights. Hari's eyes flew wide open as he covetously scanned the loot. He could feel all the years of his labour collectively stacked over each other. Each item represented his sweat, his early mornings, his late nights, the scolding, the fighting, and the bargaining. He picked up a wad and swiftly closed the safe shut, his hands shivering.

Finally, at about two in the morning, Tashi and his guest had their dinner, all drunk. The guest slowly took their leave, cue for Hari to clean up and leave.

Hari slowly closed the main door, the only entrance to the house. It clicked shut from inside.

***

It was nearly dawn. He walked briskly past the restaurant, and then he walked on and on until by daylight he had reached the outskirts of the town. By now, it was time to open the restaurant—the boys would be waiting. Hari found a truck going downhill, waved at it, and hitched a ride. It was nearing afternoon when the truck reached the hustle bustle of a border town. He handed the driver some money and made his way across the border as if disappearing into the darkness.

***

Back in Gangtok, Tashi was being carried out… only he was dead. Dead… his throat slit. A neat cut across the throat with surgical precision. A cut made by the hand of a person used to cut meat every day. The boys were all there, the police questioning them. The name "Hari" could be heard repeatedly in the police station, but no one knew where Hari was, where he was from, or even if it was his real name.

***

Hari slowly walked uphill, whistling a tune that he had heard on the radio, his breathing rapid due to exertion. The bag on his hand swayed, burdened with a heavy weight. A path was leading uphill through the jungle. Hari breathed hard, out of practice of walking in the mountainous path, his feet now strangely unsure in the narrow path through which he used to run when he was a small child. Some vague subconscious memories led him through the trail, and as he progressed, the cobweb of his mind slowly cleared.

The path gradually dipped down and turned towards the river. There was a bamboo bridge across it, and a small hamlet could be seen perched on the hilltop. Hari stopped to catch his breath and take a drink of the cool water from the stream. There was no one around, the area being sparsely populated. He rested the bag delicately on the ground just beside the flowing water and sat for a while before opening the bag.

There were bundles of notes, gold, and jewellery. Hari had grabbed some papers in the dark too while Tashi's blood made the bed sheet go red and then purple. "He was too drunk... he did not know," Hari told the soft wind blowing over the swaying bridge, wiping away his perspiration. He separated the sheets of paper and wondered what they were. Hari could not read. He looked at the papers for a long time, closed the bag, got up, and started walking across the bridge. As he reached the centre of the bridge, a huge smile on his face, he threw the papers into the flowing water and walked on.

The papers scattered over the flowing water, and within moments, the currents swiftly took them away. A paper floated for some time before reaching a rapid and smashing against the stones. A part of it came up again.

"I, Tashi in sound health and mind do hereby leave all my property including Momo shop, a house, money in the bank, and all that is legally owned by me to Hari..."

Short Story by Revathi Raj Iyer

A Girl From Siliguri

Baba, *ma*, her little half-brother and two half-sisters were blissfully asleep downstairs, in a small room separated by a large sheet of grey cloth. The entire town of Siliguri was drowned in silence. It was a cold, frosty night and the sun had hardly shone since the onset of winter, except for a few afternoons when it briefly grazed atop the mountains and disappeared quickly. Winter had shown no mercy consecutively for many years, since the meltdown of the glacier in the Himalayas. Most homes had a small fireplace of logwood, and the families huddled around it and sipped tea amidst chores, food and work. Exhaustion lulled them to sleep in spite of the harsh weather. Such was life in Siliguri, a calm, cosy town with humble, warm people who merely knew the art of survival.

The younger generation had moved away to urban areas, to seek opportunities for a better living. The older folks sought comfort during the occasional visit of their progenies who loved to come home, a break from the drudgery and demands of city life, to bask in the hills and lush plantations in which their forefathers had toiled. Their parents still sweated out just in case their children failed to send money to help them get through winter.

"Hello, hello... are you there Tisca? Please answer me." The voice of uncle Devan was fading away as the receiver slipped from her grip and dangled like a pendulum, casting a frightful shadow of a noose. Tisca shut her ears with both hands and lay curled up in bed terrified, staring at the phone in disbelief.

She had resolved to expose Vikram - attractive, wicked, garrulous and unscrupulous. She wouldn't have hesitated to plunge a knife through him, if only she had the nerve to do so. Ha! Tisca could not even harm a fly, let alone a cheat like him. She had never dreamt that her good intentions would backfire and end in such an unexpected way.

Tisca was terrified. The sheets were cold and she shivered under the cotton quilt. Her tiny space in the loft where she grew up was the same, just as depressing as her thoughts, with old heavy drapes and sparsely furnished with a bed, writing desk, a telephone which the local NGO had arranged, and tiny wooden shelves where she kept her clothes, a pair of shoe and other miscellany. Nothing had changed in Siliguri, except that her whole life was about to change, with this one phone call. The Damocles' sword could strike anytime.

What a mess she had got herself into!

***

A song under her breath and spring in her steps, nine-year old Tisca made her way homewards, after school. She was very hungry and looked forward to the daily meal of hot rice soup, bread and boiled potatoes. As she reached the corner of the street she heard loud wails. They were coming from her home and a large crowd had gathered outside. She ran faster. The gate was wide open and this was quite unusual. Her mother always made sure to close it, before she left for the fields.

Tisca paused and held onto the railing so as to catch her breath. Then she saw! A body draped in a white cloth lay outside the doorstep. Her mother, surrounded by a group of village-folk, was weeping quietly. She had never seen her mother cry. Too scared and confused Tisca stood still, school bag by her feet. She felt a tap on her shoulder. It was uncle Devan.

"When did you come?" She asked, looking up and smiling at him, in spite of the gloom. He knelt down beside her.

"*Mama*, what is wrong with *baba*? Is he sick? Is he going to God?" she asked with concern.

"Yes, he is. Your *baba's* heartbeat stopped this afternoon as he was working on the estate. My child, don't be afraid, just look at *baba*," he urged. Tisca looked at the still body of her father- peaceful, quiet as if he was fast asleep. She was not scared anymore and felt numb as the chilly wind penetrated her skin. Her *baba* was gone.

"I will see you in the evening and listen to stories about your school," were his last words that morning. Now he is gone.

"How could baba leave without saying goodbye? What will happen to me and my mother? Who will look after us? Will I be pulled out of school and made to work on the fields?" Tisca felt alone, in spite of having so many people around. She stifled her cries and pressed her face against her uncle's hands, seeking momentary comfort.

"I will take care of you," said Devan, reading his niece's mind.

***

After the funeral, Devan left for Kolkata and her mother started working on the fields.

"You must go to school tomorrow. You have stayed home for a month, Tisca. You must study and become a good girl," said her mother, as she counted the rupee notes and kept them safely in a box. Tisca nodded, noticing the look of relief on her mother's face whenever the money order arrived. Life did not change for her. She continued school and badly missed her *baba*, especially at night. He was the one who always spent time with her, every night, no matter how tired he was. He wouldn't say much but listened attentively as she rattled about her day at school, her friends and her most favourite teacher, Miss Miriam.

Two years later, her mother remarried. Tisca had a father again who looked after them just like her own *baba*. The money order stopped. The house got busy with the cries of babies, one after the other in the next four years. She now had three half-siblings. She was not their only child anymore. She missed her *baba* even more.

***

Miriam was unmarried and had joined the missionary school, since the time it was established in Siliguri. It was the duty of the teacher who took the last class, to lock the room and hand over the key to the office. Miriam was struggling with the padlock. The key was light and rusty and it took a great deal of tact to make it work.

"This is not quite a teacher's job. I must inform Prakash to make another key," Miriam muttered and marched towards the office when she noticed Tisca waiting by the corridor. There was something genuine about this girl that Miriam liked, from the very first time she had set eyes upon Tisca. She felt even more protective after her father's untimely death. Since then she had taken personal interest in Tisca's academic progress.

"You will be out of school in a few months. Have you thought about college?" Miriam asked as Tisca fell in step with her.

"I don't know madam, but I want to become a journalist," she said shyly, almost swallowing the word journalist. Miriam raised her generously bushy eyebrows at this unexpected response.

Tisca's hands flew to her mouth as she tried to suppress a smile, suddenly remembering her friend's remark. "Just imagine those eyebrows in a braid," her friend had joked, and everyone had laughed on the first day when Miss Miriam entered the class. She wasn't dumb to not understand that it was something about her, but dismissed it with a smile. Tisca was charmed by Miss Miriam's confidence and warmth.

"Did you say journalist? You have to shed a bit of your shyness, and be a brave girl. Are you ready for that?" she heard her teacher ask, with eyebrows still raised.

Tisca quickly averted her eyes and looked at the mud-stained square tiles. She kept walking with her head down. She was very fond of writing stories. The idea of becoming a journalist excited her. It was her dream to write about true life events and scoops that lay beyond the precincts of Siliguri. *"How many success stories she had read about small-town girls?"* Some of them received awards from the President. She didn't know if she could go that far, nevertheless, the very idea of writing made her happy and determined to take up journalism.

"Do you understand me, girl?" Miriam asked, as she stopped by the office.

"Yes, Miss Miriam. I will try to become brave," Tisca replied, not knowing how she was going to do that. Waving goodbye, she took the path that led to her home. "Else there was no point in wasting time and money for college," she mused and was ready to put up a fight if her step-*baba* or *man objected*. Luckily, it did not come to that.

"You can stay with uncle Devan," informed her mother, as soon as Tisca finished high school. "He will not mind at all. In fact, my brother would love to have some company, a confirmed bachelor that he is," said her mother with no expression on her face.

Tisca hadn't seen much of her uncle Devan, but remembered his money order that helped them tide through rough times, after *baba's* death. Even after her mother's remarriage, some money arrived during those lean winter months.

***

Devan worked with a regional press and was due to retire the following year. He lived in a rather isolated part of Tollygunge. It was an old house that had been renovated the year before his sister informed that Tisca would be moving in with him, for her college education. She hadn't asked for his permission. Devan loved the liberty she took back then, when he was sending the money orders, and now. As he read his sister's letter written in *Bengali*, a smile rose to his lips. She still made the same grammatical errors and her handwriting was incorrigible. *"Poor woman, no wonder had to work in the fields! What else could she have done?"* He was happy to be of some use to his sister and Tisca.

Devan meandered through the rooms, surveying every bit of the house, immensely satisfied at the timeliness of his decision to refurbish it. No more rentals. This house now belonged to him. The landlord was rushed to leave the country for good and Devan had quickly closed the deal, to his satisfaction. Having bound himself to a vow of celibacy when he had lost the woman he loved to a gory tram accident, he missed not having his own children. He was very happy to be Tisca's guardian. She was like a daughter to him.

"It all seemed like yesterday that she came to stay with me. How time flies," he thought as Tisca stood before him full of smiles. She was flaunting her graduation certificate, still shy but more confident.

"You must enroll for Masters," Devan began, but Tisca interrupted him.

"I have already and not just that, I also have a job as a trainee in mid-eastern daily with field responsibilities after six months," she said, with exuberance.

"When did my little niece get so bold, confident and clever? Doesn't this call for a special treat?" Devan asked, as he opened the refrigerator and brought out the dish of *rosgullas*.

"Let me call *ma* and *baba* and give them the good news," said Tisca and sprinted to her room.

"Make it quick girl," he groaned, eyeing the delectable white balls floating in sugar syrup lightly coated with saffron.

"I will," she hollered little knowing that in less than a year, her whole life was going to change.

***

It had begun with Lolita. This was around the time when Tisca had just moved to this dreary old city.

"A female company and a new friend is precisely what my niece needs," Devan felt in order to help Tisca come out of her cocoon. Lolita worked in the same press and he told her all about Tisca, her childhood and her days in Siliguri.

"Tisca is shy and has trouble making friends here," he added.

"Devan *da*, I do understand. I will come home this Sunday," said the ever obliging Lolita, affable by nature and a Kolkatan at heart. Much to his relief, the girls got along like a house on fire. In no time their friendship grew and got to the point where Tisca started to feel possessive about Lolita. She felt a stab of envy whenever Lolita rattled about her other friends, a feeling unknown to herself, a strange obsession that spelt doom, which she failed to realise.

On this dark night at Siliguri, the very thought of Lolita made her cringe. She sobbed into her pillows uncontrollably, as she remembered that unfortunate day when Vikram had set his eyes on Lolita.

"If only I could turn the clock back," she thought remorsefully.

***

"Dowdy, but smart," that stuck in her mind like glue. Tired of being mocked at her looks and timidity, Tisca had taken Lolita to office to proudly 'show off' her best friend to her colleagues at work, to send a message across that even the dowdiest can have a beautiful friend.

"Who is this lovely lady?" asked Vikram who had walked past, but quickly retraced his steps after seeing Lolita.

"Tisca, will you not introduce me to your friend?" he said with growing impatience.

Vikram was her boss and well-known to be flirty with pretty girls. Reluctantly, Tisca introduced Lolita and Vikram. Their handshake seemed to last forever. Feeling stupid and embarrassed Tisca mumbled something inaudible and both stepped back, still gazing at each other. Their chemistry had clicked instantly. In less than a week Lolita informed that she was seeing Vikram.

"No way, how did it all happen? You never told me," she responded in an accusing tone. Tisca was hurting and deep down she knew that the damage was done. Vikram was a charmer and had effortlessly hypnotised the gullible Lolita, who was smitten by the attention showered upon her.

"These things happen quickly," said Lolita. "You wouldn't understand," she added.

That hurt even more. "Please stop this nonsense. Vikram is not a good man," she pleaded.

"Don't be silly and no need to get motherly," said Lolita, and dismissed her concern with a friendly shrug.

Two months later, Lolita flaunted her engagement ring. Tisca was shocked and disturbed that her friend was madly and rapturously in love with the most atrocious man, to make it worse.

"I have to do something. All this was getting out of hand," she fumed.

In the meanwhile, Lolita's visit to uncle Devan's place became less frequent. "What is the matter, Tis? Why is Loli not coming these days?" Devan had this funny habit of shortening names, which she otherwise loved, but not that day.

"Lolita is engaged," she informed sullenly.

"Well, no wonder, then. Who is the lucky man? Have you met him? Invite them to our house," said Devan cheerfully. "Now that I am retired and as you know spend most of my time reading, I look forward to visitors and chatter at home," he added in his usual good-humored way.

"My foot," thought Tisca. "I don't know yet. Sure, I will invite them both if you insist," she said flatly.

***

One day, Tisca was finishing up an interview with a florist, well known for her exotic flowers imported from Southeast Asia, when she saw Vikram at a jewellery shop located on the opposite side. He was with a woman who seemed to be in her early forties and looked much older than Lolita, even from that distance she could tell.

"Who on earth was she?" Tisca's heart started pounding faster. Acknowledging the florist's profuse gratitude with a smile and nod, she stuffed her notes inside the bag and stepped out in the mid-morning heat. She took a few giant steps and ducked under the semi-tattered awning of a crowded hawker place selling *puchkas* and lemon *sherbet*.

"I have to find out who this woman is and alert Lolita." She watched them closely. The woman was talking animatedly and Vikram had his arm around her. Finally, Tisca saw the woman select something, a bracelet or necklace, it was hard to tell. *"Or was it a ring?"*

The heat and humidity suddenly made her nauseous. She felt a strange sensation in the pit of her stomach, at the manner in which the woman was articulating. She was almost certain this woman was Vikram's wife. Instinct warned her to back off but she was unable to stop herself. Tisca surreptitiously clicked a photo of them. Determined to find out the truth, she walked inside the store exactly twenty minutes after they left. A tactful chat confirmed her suspicion. The woman *was* his wife and she *had* chosen a pearl necklace as an anniversary gift. Tisca loitered around feigning interest and when nobody was looking, she slipped out wasting no time to forward the photo to Lolita.

"This should drill some sense in you. I ought to be on the investigation team rather than being sent to interview florists," she muttered as she headed towards the office.

***

Lolita was at the hair salon when she heard the beep. She stared in disbelief at the photo for a few minutes. Tisca's message read - "Be careful, he is slimy. When confronted, even a snake recoils, before lashing out." She left the salon and got into her car.

"Vikram, meet me in ten minutes at the usual place. This is urgent."

Even before he could respond, she had disconnected. He knew that something was terribly wrong and it had to do with him. He had barely reached his desk when Lolita's abrupt call had come through.

"What else could be urgent at this time of the day? Could she have spotted me at the jewellery store?" he wondered. As he hurried past the hallway again, he noticed that Tisca's chair was unoccupied. He felt uneasy but had no time to ask around.

"No big deal. I will confess and turn on my charm, not a big problem with girls like Lolita," he assured himself as the engine roared into action.

Lolita was waiting at their usual café. Vikram had an uncanny feeling that she knew everything. "*How could she have found out? If she had spotted him at the jewellery store, she would have stormed in."* Vikram sat opposite to her pondering if he should confess straight away.

"I am waiting for Vikram." Lolita broke into his thoughts. He was right. She knew.

"Oh, okay. Well, I want you to listen carefully and honestly to God I didn't mean to deceive you. I love you and want to marry you." He paused. Lolita sat like a stone with a frozen look on her face.

"That woman is my wife. She is a government officer in Delhi and comes to Kolkata once in a while. We are soon getting a divorce. The jewellery was a ploy to keep her in good humour so that we part amicably."

"What else are you hiding from me?" demanded Lolita, her stony face giving way to some life.

Taking advantage of this, he said with a pretentious gush of emotion, "It is not what you think. I have no children."

Lolita was taken aback with his upfront confession. Although upset, furious and fully prepared to break her engagement, she weakened and decided to give him another chance. Vikram was overjoyed that his charm worked no matter how difficult the situation was.

Tisca was anxiously waiting for the call and jumped at the first ring.

"Have you both split up?" she asked eagerly. Tisca was beyond words when she heard Lolita say that

Vikram was man enough to confess, and she was going to give him another chance.

"How could you be so foolish? Can you not see through his lies? He is simply leading you on," she wanted to argue. But she remained silent. It was of no use at all. Tisca was hurt and at the same time felt responsible for the trap that Lolita was getting into. There was no way she could work with Vikram, anymore. It wouldn't be too long before he found out that she was the one spying on him.

She made up her mind to go back to Siliguri, although she didn't have the faintest idea of what she would do there. The next morning, she informed Devan. "Uncle, I am homesick. I have been thinking of going back to Siliguri for a few days."

Much to her relief, he readily agreed. "You have not met *ma*, *baba* and your siblings, in ages. When did I become so selfish? When do you want to leave? I will make all the arrangements." Tisca hadn't quite expected this and felt extremely grateful.

Devan knew that there was something more to it, than being homesick. Tisca had avoided looking at him, when she spoke. She was hiding something from him. *"Was it a boy?"* He wondered. Tisca felt a tad guilty for not being forthright with her caring uncle. Although she was tempted to tell him the truth, she held back. It was pointless.

***

Back in Siliguri, with nothing much to do, Tisca decided to meet Miss Miriam. As she was idling in the office she flipped through the newspaper. There was an advertisement for a nanny. Her heart skipped a beat as her glance fell upon the last line - "Please contact Ms. Sadhana Vikram Bose, Under Secretary."

"That lying, treacherous bastard!" Drawing in a sharp breath she folded the paper, tucked it under her arm and hurried back home without meeting Miss Miriam.

That night Tisca began writing a story, a true story - a revelation. She addressed the envelope to Ms. Sadhana Vikram Bose. This was her one last attempt to save Lolita from the clutches of Vikram.

***

Sadhana Vikram Bose had doubts about her husband's fidelity. This story had fallen in her lap, like a godsend. She looked with disdain at the photos of Vikram and the other woman. The envelope bore the stamp of Siliguri. There was no address or name of the sender. That hardly mattered as there were more important things to attend to.

***

Later one night, Devan was watching the news, his daily routine after dinner. There seemed nothing interesting. As he was about to switch off the television, he heard something that sent tremors through his entire body. He watched in disbelief as he shuffled through the news channels. The remote fell limply on the carpet. His thoughts raced to Tisca.

Devan's hands were unsteady as he dialed his sister's number. It took a long time to connect and the line was feeble. His voice shook as he spoke to his dear niece, who was more than a daughter to him.

"Tisca, my child," and his voice faltered but Tisca could hear the breaking news:

"A brilliant editor of mid-eastern daily, Mr. Vikram Bose was found dead in his apartment with his fiancé, Lolita, this evening ..."

Tisca recoiled in terror and the receiver slipped.

"Hello, hello, are you there Tisca? Please answer me," the voice of uncle Devan echoed repeatedly in the darkness of the night.

***

Glossary

Baba	father
Bengali	language of West Bengal
Da	elder brother
Ma	mother
Mama	maternal uncle
Puchkas	tangy snack also known as Pani Puris
Rosgullas	syrupy dessert with cottage cheese balls
Sherbet	cooling drink

Poem by Harinder Cheema

The Tale of a Crying City

A City of concrete jungle covered with smog

Where apathy is the attitude and people are as dead as the log

A City where I yearn to see the clear blue sky

The air space is usurped by the flying machines where once the birds used to fly

A City of fast lanes

A City of the metro trains

A City of fake profiles

A City of plastic smiles

A City of people, corrupt

Unethical and morally bankrupt

A City with the tales of crime

A City that has no time

To care, share or live in brotherhood

A City that needs to learn a lesson from a Village about the things , good

A City that never sleeps

Everywhere one finds huge garbage heaps

A City not safe for women

A City where the calm of the night is disturbed by the noise often

A City with amenities many but no peace

A City where water is also available for some fees

A City of contrasts

Of the rich in the pubs and hotels and also of the struggling middle class

A City that is not ashamed of its slums

A City with a cold heart and a body numb

A City which burns in the heat and gets clogged in the rain

A City that needs psychiatrists to keep the people sane

This is the tale of my crying City

That was ravaged of its natural beauty.

Short Story by Barnali Basu

Say You Love Me

"Preeti? Preeti? Hello?"

"Huh?"

"What's the matter with you? Where are you lost?" Aryan demanded, annoyed.

Preeti blushed hard and muttered softly, "I'm sorry…."

Chastened, he smiled, "Exams are approaching in 2 months, and you are perpetually lost in dreams. We have to pay attention." He began to turn the pages onto the next chapter.

And how does one do that when the source of distraction is sitting beside you? That square face, dark black eyes, sharp features, wavy hair had been holding her hostage for the past two weeks.

She hadn't felt this way before. Aryan and she had known each other since first year. Their friendship had been further cemented when they discovered they lived close to each other. While all the other girls in their class had crushes of varying degrees on him from the very start, he had been nothing more than a study pal to her. They hardly talked much except to exchange notes or in group chats. It's only during exams that they had this one-to-one time with each other for detailed studying. It was however, now in their final year that she seemed to be discovering this whole new side of him. And hers as well.

It was not just about his looks. It was also about the way he walked, the way he talked, just the way he carried himself around. Every move of his was swathed in style. And the way he smiled. Her heartbeats quickened at the sight of that charming grin. Preeti had met many men, but Aryan Raichura was different. And what she had begun to feel for him was way different.

She had started exasperating him, she could see that. By staying lost in her dreams about him while all he wanted to do was focus on the upcoming exams. But her heart was allowing anything but that.

I don't know what's happening to me…. All I think about is him, all I see is him, all I want is him. Does he think about me in the same way too? Does he want to take me in his arms when his heart cries out? Does he want to sit with me on the rooftop and count the stars? Does he think I am the most beautiful woman in the world? Does he feel he cannot live without me? Does he…....

"For Goodness sake, Preeti, what is the matter with you? "Aryan nearly shouted now. "What the hell are you thinking?" Preeti looked at him a little shyly then smiled, "I am thinking…I was thinking …I think I love you…"

"Hi Aryan!!!" Preeti cackled loudly and waved her hand madly at him. Aryan grimaced and placed his head on the canteen table. "Don't worry Aryan. Preeti Bhargav is not the first girl to have fallen in love with you." Sanjeev Chanana sitting next to him muttered. "She is just the most persistent one!" Megha Dahiya completed it. The table of twelve burst out in unison.

Aryan made a face. The creepiest one would be more like it. Seriously, whenever he laid eyes on that girl with those globular questioning eyes, always messed up brown hair, protuberant belly accentuated by those baggy T-shirts and pants she always wore and that permanently surprised expression, he had a hard time believing she was the topper of his class. And that jarring laughter of hers, oh God, enough to scare away a group of ogres. He had only befriended her as he needed to pass with decent marks so that he could apply for further education abroad. Nothing more, nothing less. But now, she had developed this crush on him and was irritating him day and night. He already suffered for her company for the sake of his grades, but her antics were now becoming intolerable.

"Aryan! Aryan!" She had reached him by now, "You know I had the wildest dream about us!!" "Oh yeah?" Sanjeev chimed in, "What did you see?" "I saw us on a ship bound for heaven. Just you and me. Together." She beamed in delight. "And I left you there and came back, didn't I? "Aryan said sarcastically, got up and left. Preeti stood watching dejectedly as others started to guffaw.

Aryan looked at the four page long poem in his hand, making a strong effort not to scream. This was the tenth or twelfth love gift he had received from that annoying Preeti by now. It had been a card yesterday, a bottle of cologne a few days back and gosh a small teddy bear a week back! Nearly every day a new embarrassment lay waiting on his college desk. Not that there was any respite in the remaining hours of the day. She kept sending him lovey dovey SMSs and mandatorily called him up each night to wish him sweet dreams. The only moment she seemed to sober up was ironically the time that had started it all, their study time together when he sternly reminded them that their semester exams were approaching. How long would he have to bear this torture? Can't this girl understand when he said it once he was not in the least interested in her?

With a snarl, he tore the papers and hurled the pieces into the nearby dustbin. At a desk some distance from him, Preeti watched the scene wistfully but smiled, nevertheless.

I know it has been a bit of a surprise for you which is why you are acting up. But once you realize we are meant to be together, you will come to me of your own accord. I will keep trying my very best. I will not give up no matter what. I will make you love me just the way I love you.

"Preeti, we need to talk". Preeti's smile faded at the tone of his voice. Looks like he had not liked her gift this time too. She blushed and nodded at him. "No, not here" he reached out and grabbed her wrist. She winced in pain at his strong grip, but he paid no heed and pulled her up and out of the canteen in almost one swoop.

"You did this, didn't you?" He waved the notebook at her face after he had dragged her out of the college building at a secluded spot. She looked shamefacedly at him. Even she had had a doubt that lacing the margins of his notebook with love quotes was going a bit too far. Clearly it was. She had never seen him this furious ever before.

"I meant you well Aryan," she began weakly. "I did too until now," he bore down upon her," which is why I kept tolerating this nonsense. But not anymore. You are the most intelligent girl of this class, aren't you? You know all the fundas of IT like the back of your hand? And you can't understand plain simple English? That my answer to you is No, Noni, Naaaah?"

She cowered in fright, her lips quivering, "Besides, what on earth made you think I will ever say yes to you? Have you looked at yourself in the mirror? The college beauty queen proposed to me and I said no! "She had known this argument would be thrown at her someday, "I know I am no match for all the kinds of girls that are behind you Aryan, but," she added firmly, "Nobody can ever love you the way I do." "To hell with you and your love," He screeched angrily, making her flinch. He narrowed his eyes at her almost as the raging bull charging at a matador, "The only reason I was friends with you was that you helped me with studies, and you have failed at that front too. I have barely managed to scrape through the semester exams. What! Oh my God! She looked at him alarmed. "You have destroyed my peace of mind, my sleep and appetite and now you are out to destroy my life too!" He growled. She shook her head starting to shiver when he pushed her away from him, "I never liked you but now I hate you. If you ever come near me again, I swear you've had it!" He glared at her and walked away.

"I guess that solves your problem about that psycho bitch," Sanjeev patted him on the back. Aryan grimaced, "You know what they say about dog tails, "the other girls at the canteen table giggled, "She has stopped with her stupid gifts but still keeps calling. I don't pick up, blocked her number on my cell but she keeps buzzing on the landline, that stupid oaf! Oh God here she comes, "he hurriedly got up as he spotted a worried looking Preeti at the canteen entrance, "Guys I'm leaving. Take care of her." And he was off.

Preeti looked around and came up to the table. Her hair was all disheveled and her eyes looked like she hadn't slept for days, "Sanjeev! Sanjeev!" She frantically asked, "Where is Aryan? Have you seen him?" "Well yes." "Where is he?" "He has left for Nainital.He plans to stay with his grandparents for study leave." Preeti was flabbergasted. "Nainital? But why?" "You have only yourself to thank for that,"

He replied sternly, "He nearly failed the semesters thanks to you. He wants to at least pass the finals decently." Preeti stood rooted at her spot for a moment then slowly said, "Do you have his contact number there?" "I do but he has strictly told us not to give it to you. Please Preeti because of you, our friend has left us and gone. Please don't disturb him anymore. Let him stay in peace." Aryan rejoined the table after she had left and everyone had a hearty laugh together.

Preeti sadly entered her room and flung her bag on the study table. She sat on the chair and buried her face in her hands.

What have I done? I forgot love was all about ushering happiness in someone's life. To think about his joys and pleasures. And like a selfish prick I only thought about myself, my wishes, and my needs. I should have accepted defeat gracefully and moved away but thanks to my stupidity, I have not only kicked out my best friend and the only man I ever loved out of my life but also pushed his life at the brink of disaster.

"Shit!" She spat out again and again, "Shit! Shit!" Aryan was right. She never deserved him. Ever.

I didn't think I would ever fall in love again. I know that everyone says that after a heartbreak, but the difference is that I'm not heartbroken. I'm not cynical, or pessimistic, or sad. I'm just someone who once felt something bigger than anything else I'd ever felt and when I lost it, I honestly believed I would never have that again. But... I was 22 then and life is long. And I'm feeling things right now that I haven't in a long, long time.

Preeti had just got a glimpse and was straining hard for a better look when she felt a hand on her shoulder. "Yes, yes, Preeti, that was Aryan. The very Aryan you scared away during college," Gurleen said teasingly causing the other girls sitting around to bubble into a giggle together. She blushed and then straightened up," Yeah right, "she muttered. She had found the truth of that lie some years down the line.

"He's still quite the catch, "remarked Neetu flippantly. "But way beyond yours," Shabri nicked her on the forehead, "Don't you know he is a celebrity lawyer now earning in millions?" "And married," Rita chimed in, "And if I've heard right, his wife was a Miss India finalist." Preeti sighed as all the girls ooed collectively. Gurleen was called in just then and all conversation ceased.

Preeti sat happily; sipping on a cold drink and watching the festive mood all around her as women beat on a drum and sang folk songs. Men and women were dancing on the thumps, some of them her friends from college days. Amid it all sat the radiant bride Gurleen getting mehndi applied on her hands.

It was indeed on occasions like these that so many people so far apart came back together, she reflected as she looked at her friends and how much had changed in these 7 years.Some were fatter, some thinner, some balder. Some married and some with kids.

Nearly everybody was here. Except for Megha who was battling a bitter divorce settlement with her abusive husband and Sanjeev who had died 8 months back of lung cancer. She had not been sure if Aryan would come but here he was.

She started to tap her foot softly as another rocking number resounded. It had been a wedding like this that had changed the course of her life forever when she had been dazzled by the jewellery displayed all around. Her father had not been too pleased at her decision to take up the course but now he was proud of her. Her designs had become the talk of the town in no time and were coveted by some of the richest and wealthiest families of the country. Even Gurleen's fiancé had paid lavishly to cover for all the four days.

Ironically, she had no intentions of becoming the center of a similar event for herself. Her parent's nagging had made her shift base to Delhi promptly. Not that she was against the institution, but she felt no need for it. Until now.

She was laughing and chatting with her friends as they walked back to the guest house they had been put up in when she spotted Aryan again. He was walking in the opposite direction towards the hall without as much as a glance at them. Slyly she removed herself from the group, turned back and started to follow him. He had covered a lot of distance ahead and she had to literally start running to keep pace with him.

She had reached the side of a shrubbery when she tripped on her ghaghra. She would have had a nasty fall when a pair of hands grabbed her. She found herself looking into the smiling blue eyes of Aarav Chopra, the bride's cousin and blushed. This was the fourth time he had caught her from falling. "You knew I was here?" He teased me." Yeah no wonder I fell". She grinned and nodded.

She finally reached the hall but found him chatting and drinking with a group of men.

The songs the DJ was belting out in the pre-wedding night bash were simply irresistible. Preeti had a hard time keeping her feet off the floor getting ample support from the bride and her friends. Suddenly she saw Aryan's wife come and join them. That meant....

After much searching in the soft darkness, she found him seated with some others. She was about to call out to him when she heard the scrap of conversation going on, "She was quite a thing wasn't she?" "A thing? Quite a dumbo she was. Gifted me a teddy bear. I mean who does that? I tell you toppers are idiots in real life." Preeti walked away silently.

The wedding turned out to be a real grand affair and a resounding success on all counts. Everybody was praising her designs and Preeti was beside herself with happiness. The pheras were over and the couple was seated at the royal chairs for people to wish them. Preeti was walking towards the entrance when she saw Aryan walking towards her. He looked even more handsome, the grey of his temples adding to a touch of wisdom to his looks. Smiling widely, she approached him when he simply walked past her, his gaze fixed on the just married couple.

"Hey babe!" Preeti turned to find Harry, the bride's brother walking towards her. She quickly averted her face and tried gliding off, but he had reached her. "Come on babe, "he grabbed her arm, "Come let's have a nightcap". Feeling nauseated by the smell of whisky, she somehow managed, "Look Harry. You're drunk. Go home." "Oh, come on…" he would have fallen on her, but she stopped him. He began to wrap his arms around her when she screamed and pushed him away. "You bitch!" He lunged furiously at her when a pair of hands grabbed him. "When the girl says no, she means it." Aarav said tersely. So, the muscles he flaunted in his TV serial we're not just for show, Preeti noted as he shoved the totally stoned fellow to the ground who then passed out immediately. The event left her shaken though. She didn't protest as the hero of the moment offered her a ride back home.

"I hope that the rascal didn't hurt you. When he gets drunk, he thinks he is the King and the world is his subject." He smiled at her as they drove down the empty dark street. She smiled back, "Nothing much ,I……" she froze mid-sentence as a black Mercedes whooshed past them, Aryan and his wife grinning at each other inside.

"Aryan?"

"Yes?" Aryan turned and froze. "I have been looking for you throughout the wedding. Finally caught you at the reception. Remember me? Preeti Bhargav? The girl who scared you from college?"

Remember her? Aryan wondered if he was dreaming. This nimble creature with an hourglass figure, round kohl lined black eyes, lush long hair, and rosy lips with a quiet grace, resplendent in a shiny purple lehenga was?

"Actually, I have been meaning to say this to you for quite some time. Right from that day in the canteen when you.. er.... left. But I never got the chance. I want to apologize to you for the way I behaved with you. I should have understood it when you had said no. I mean what's there to think. No means no, doesn't it?" She laughed nervously.

Wait a minute. He had said no to her? This woman is ten times more gorgeous than his wife? He had been getting the buzz of the jewellery designer dazzling everyone with both her work and personality.But she had been her? "They do say we tend to act a little crazy in love and I was in that phase then." She gave a sheepish laugh, "I hope I have not really caused you much damage and wish you all the very best in life."

Aryan was still in a trance as the angel-like figure shook his hand and stalked away. The memories of the cackling, cretinous girl bubbling around him, hiding shyly behind her desk as he inspected her gifts with derision , making googly eyes at him as they studied together ran over his mind in a motion picture. Who had been the idiot all along he wondered as he trudged on to the raucous call of his wife inside the hall, prepared for the umpteenth time to get a tongue lashing for speaking to a woman.

Finally, I got it off my chest. I have finally put the past behind me. I can move forward now. All ready for the future.

Preeti was shimmying with her girlfriends when Aarav walked up to her and put out his hand. "May I have the pleasure of this dance?"

Aryan was struggling to keep pace with his annoyed wife while throwing glances like everyone at the most good-looking couple on the dance floor. Preeti was ensconced in Aarav's arms, smiling in his eyes, gliding along to the rhythm. "What are you thinking?" He asked her.

That's the problem of the human mind. Howmuchever you promise you won't make the same mistake again, it still makes you do it.

"I think," she said, "I love you."

Short Story by Tulika Majumder

The Transition

"Ma'am – it is the same modus operandi, the head is smashed and a number is stuck on the wall if the room- this time it is 4 (four) ... the previous three times we got 1, 2, and 3 respectively" - Sub-Inspector Naskar stopped for a while as Lajwanti Lahiri - DCP Homicide Department, sat quietly listening to him on the other side of the table. She tapped her pen on the table and said, "Didn't we any tissues recovered for forensics?" "No" Vasudev Naskar shook his head. Kolkata Police Homicide Department was in real trouble this time. This was the fourth murder in the last one month and each victim was been killed in exactly the same way. At first, it was not clearly established as pattern, but after the 3rd incident there was no room for any doubt. There was definitely a serial killer at large in the heart of Kolkata! The Homicide Department was yet to make a breakthrough and so far there has been no progress apart from establishing a pattern. Yesterday, DC DD had called Lajwanti and put a lot of pressure on her to make arrests. It was true that police had no specific clues or leads to follow. Not even forensics were able to report anything outstanding. The media was going berserk over the events and unfortunately, the "murderer/murderers" committed the murders with due caution ensuring no loose evidence was left behind. The victims were not that well-known, although all were established in their lives and careers. All of them were aged between 40 and 45 and were residents of Kolkata for generations. Apart from this fact, there was no link or commonality between them that would establish a motive or pattern of a typical serial killing. Veteran police officer Lajwanti's forehead sported a deep furrow ever since the departmental pressure started coming her way to conclude the case. After sub-inspector Naskar left the room, Lajwanti sat down with a paper and pencil to arrange the events in chronological order. This was an old habit learnt from her seniors in her IPS training. Whenever she lost trail of events, she resorted to the old method of pencil and paper. In her career of thirteen years, she had not faced such roadblock often. Lajwanti arranged the information of the 4 victims in detail following the method taught by her mentor Atulya Munsi, a former Homicide Branch Head. It went as below:

1 - Sanjay Tarafdar – Bengali by origin, house in Chetla, age 43 years, by profession a businessman, childless and divorced for the last 8 years. He lived alone. His former wife was currently a resident of Patna. Divorce was consensual so there was less possibility of a secret enmity related to it. According to the employees at his factory, they were not aware of any business rivalry involving their proprietor. The date of the murder was May 12th around 10 pm. The murder came to light the next day when the maid came to work. There was a piece of paper written in

English stuck on the wall of the room. It mentioned the digit "1".

2 - Sanklan Ghosh – Bengali by origin, age 45 years, resident of Lake Town, employed. The son studied in a residential school in Karsiong. Sanklan Ghosh himself was a former student of that school. Wife Anusuya Ghosh was a housewife but spent most of her time at "Karsiong parents stay in hostel" attached to her son's school. It was known that the relationship between husband and wife was "normal" with no reported tensions. The date of the murder was 17th May between 9 pm and 11 pm. The wife was in Karsiong on the day of the murder. The murder came to light a day later when his wife called a neighbor since she was not being able to reach him on the phone for past 24 hours. There was a piece of paper written in English stuck on the wall of the room. It mentioned the digit "2".

3 - Rajendra Yadav – Bihari by origin, age 43 years. Resident of Kolkata for 3 generations. He belonged to a business family and lived in Park Circus. He was not married and lived with his aged parents. The date of murder was May 23 between 12 pm and 3 am. At the time of the murder, the parents were at home, but they lived on the second floor, so they did not hear or realized anything. The murder came to light the next afternoon when the victim's father came downstairs to look for his son. There was a piece of paper stuck on the wall of the room which mentioned the digit "3".

4 - Jyotish Sen - Bengali NRI, living in Canada, Age 43 years. Was staying in his house at Elliot Road, for 2 months since he came for his yearly vacation to India. Wife was Canadian, had not accompanied him. He and his attendant only lived in the house. The date of murder was May 26 between 10 pm and 2.30 am. The murder was discovered the next morning when the attendant who slept on a different floor came to serve bed tea to him. There was a piece of paper stuck on the wall of the room with the digit "4" written on it.

In all the 4 cases, no motive or cause of murder could be established through interrogation, and Forensics also could not find any foreign tissue that could lead to any identification of the assailant. All the incidents occurred when the victims were alone and no one heard any noise or were alerted. The pieces of paper were stuck with common glue (had no fingerprints) and the scribbling was with a common felt permanent marker in calligraphic style, so no handwriting pattern could also be recorded.

Lajwanti went through the victim list again and again with her hand supporting her forehead and tried to find any commonality or connections between the murder incidents – this was again a method taught method taught to her by Atulya Munsi. However, apparently, nothing was evident except for the similarity between their age group and city of residence. It was already 8 o'clock, so Lajwanti got up to go home. Before leaving she called sub-inspector

Naskar and said "We are missing something Naskar" tomorrow first hour I want some more information about these four people. Where did they go in the last few months, what were their addictions, circle of friends, hobbies...etc. , you know what I mean! ..there has to be a common angle between all of these, I am certain!". The conviction in her voice was too apparent to her reportee at the other end of the table.

The car was running towards Lake Gardens but Lajwanti was constantly thinking about the events of "numerical serial killing" as the media called these incidents lately. Suddenly her phone rang. Lajwanti looked at the phone and saw a Facebook notification. A teammate from her IPS batch of 1985 had posted something. As she kept looking at the phone screen, Lajwanti's jaw tightened! How could she miss such a common thing – she despaired! Lajwanti immediately called Sub-Inspector Naskar on speed dial. "Madam!" Naskar's voice sounded a bit surprised! "Listen! Immediately check all the social media accounts of these 4 victims. Loop in Anirban from Cyber Cell.. "I need a complete sheet on their profiles"! Lajwanti hung up the phone once she let out the crisp orders. she had reached her home, now was her "me" time and she needed to think really hard!

The next day at 10 am when Lajwanti entered her office, she saw Anirban Laha of Cyber Cell and Sub-Inspector Naskar sitting in the room, waiting for her. As she entered, the two stood up and greeted together "Good morning madam"! The brightness of their eyes and faces were telltale and Lajwanti understood that her guess had hit the mark. The missing link was probably detailed in the papers they held in their hands. Lajwanti rang the bell, ordered three cups of red tea and then looked at the couple seated on the other side of the desk and said "Tell me". "Madam, look, I have managed to open the Facebook account of 3 out of the 4 victims. Sanklan Babu's account may have been deleted by him but the findings are very positive" Anirban gave the sheaf of papers to Lajwanti Besides the Facebook profile snap of 3 victims, comparative notes with a red pen were scribbled. Lajwanti's eyes brightened - " St. Patrick School – Karseong " – she murmured. Check In " 3rd October 2011 at St. Patrick Alumnus Meet – the note read.

Missing Link was found! A very potent link indeed! Lajwanti looked at sub-inspector Naskar and said "Naskar you and I would travel by train tonight. Book the ticket and take an appointment from the Principal". She then smiled and looked at Anirban before congratulating the young man. "Well Done" – lipped Lajwanti. Sub-inspector Naskar shook his head and said, "Okay, madam, I am booking tickets for Kanchankanya express tonight. But I needed to add one more thing that though Sanklan Babu's Facebook profile was not found but during our investigation I found out that his son studies in St. Patrick School only!" Lajwanti was satisfied, "the climax is approaching", her beaming face seemed to say.

The traditional British architecture sitting in the lap of the hill was a sight guaranteed to mellow hearts. When Lajwanti crossed the gate of St. Patrick School and stepped towards the principal's room, she thought to herself "what a paradox to come to such a beautiful place only to find the source of such a heinous crime". Principal Mr Aubrey Gregory Rosedale was a very bright middle-aged second-generation Irishman. Once they exchanged pleasantries, he said "Madam I came to this school in September 2012 so I can't help you much on your mission but our Geography teacher Alkesh Samanta is an alumnus of this school only and also the sitting Alumnus President - I shall call him, I'm sure he can help."

Alkesh Samanta was 40-45 years old and a very heavy looking man. At first, he was a little surprised to see Lajwanti, but after hearing the reason behind her visit, his face showed a strong expression of hatred! " Look madam it is not acceptable to kill someone under any circumstances, but I would say they might have suffered the consequences of their own karma" | Lajwanti was bemused and said " Like…?" Alkesh took a long breath and started his monologue "I knew all 4 of them. We all were only one or two years apart in our ages and batches of this school. However, whatever they did during the school reunion a few years back took the alumni days to handle the aftermath. Nandan, the 15-year-old son of Raghuvir, the janitor of our school for many years, was doing odd jobs for us that year and helping us arrange stuff.

Nandan was a student of this school only and had earned a scholarship. He was a very bright boy. We were paying him some money against the services rendered. Rajen Pandey, had made Nandan buy liquor and opium from local sellers and the other three had joined him for consuming the same. Once they got intoxicated and out of control, they asked Nandan to arrange some local girls for them. Nandan was shocked at their demand and protested. These 3 men, on being thwarted in their intentions, started beating him so much that Nandan fainted. He was lying unconscious in the backyard of the school when we found him the next day after Raghubir informed us that Nandan had not returned home last night. The boy recovered but could not speak for a long time out of shock. Then do you know what happened? One day the boy ran away from home – we don't know where he went but he simply went missing. We could not face Raghubir for a long time after this incident out of shame. Raghubir, pining for his only child died last year. We had not filed a police complaint as the committee had not wanted any controversy around this but we debarred all 4 of them from the alumni group for lifetime." As Lajwanti sat listening to Alkesh Samanta, an outline of probable murder motive was taking shape in her mind. Aloud she asked Alkesh the location of Nandan's house and if anybody lived in the house these days?" Alkesh said that the house was in a quaint area near "Engineer Patti" but no one lived in the house as they had no other relatives. Lajwanti stood up and thanked Alkesh Samanta. She needed to go to Nandan's house once.

Lajwanti asked to stop the car at a tea shop on the way to the "Engineer Patti" - the intention was to talk to some locals who were sitting there, drinking tea and gossiping. Seeing Lajwanti in uniform, a man came forward and asked "Madam, kuch hua hai kya?" The man's name was Shyamsunder, and he was the local postman. He looked very confused when he was asked about Raghuvir and shook his head. Then he related in broken hindi with a heavy North Bengal local accent which basically meant Raghuvir was a very simple man. Ever since Nandan ran away from home his physical condition continued to deteriorate and finally he died last year. The house had been lying vacant for a long time but someone moved in a month ago – the locals presumed Raghuvir had sold his house for money, before he died. They did not know who lived there, but there was a household helper in that house, who ran all house chores. No one knew the current owner. Lajwanti started calculating quickly, the pieces of the puzzle were slowly coming together. They took the directions to the house and drove towards a hilly area a little away from the main road that ran through the "Engineer Patti".

It was a wooden house, similar to normal houses in the area. The windows were closed. One had to cross a small balcony to reach the door. Lajwanti stood in front of the door and Sub-Inspector Naskar knocked on it in brisk knocks. Thirty seconds later a short stout man opened the door. He looked like he hailed from the west of the country. Upon seeing the newcomers, he raised his eyebrows and asked, "Aplog koun?" Sub-Inspector Naskar introduced himself and told them they were there to meet the owner of the house. The man looked strangely annoyed but considering their uniforms he seemed to waver and asked them to take a seat in the front room. He went inside to call his master. Lajwanti entered the house and started inspecting the room minutely. The room was very clean with only one picture hanging from the wall. Lajwanti was watching the photo frame intently when a woman's voice spoke from behind "Aplog mujhse milan chahte the?"Lajwanti quickly turned round and saw a young woman of age 23-24 years standing in front of her. She had a pretty face with slightly mongolian features and looked like a localite. She wore a t-shirt and a pair of denims clad her legs. Lajwanti had not exactly expected to meet a lady! She had a strong gut feeling that it would be Nandan whom they would find here, maybe in some disguise. She quickly recovered from her initial reaction and introduced herself to the young lady and asked, "Apka naam jaan sakte hai". "Sonika Pradhan" came the reply in a gentle tone. Aap kya ye makan kharide ho " - Sub-Inspector Naskar asked | " Jee nahi, ye mere pitajika ghar hai ".... Sub-Inspector Naskar was stunned for a moment. Sonika continued " I speak Bengali too - please sit down, I am asking Bhushan to bring some tea." She sat on the sofa and asked "that picture on the wall...?" – she left the question purposely incomplete. Sonika replied "That is my late father Raghuvir Pradhan and my late brother Nandan Pradhan. Did you want to meet for any special reason? No one knows that I am here...in fact no one knows much about me. I was only 3 years old when my uncle had taken me away to Mumbai where I grew up. I wanted to come here for some time after my father passed away, that's why you found me here." Lajwanti was a little confused at how smoothly Sonika related her story.

But during her long career with the police if she had learnt something it was that nothing should be taken for granted. Moreover, if not Nanda, his sister was no less a suspect – the motive of revenge on her brother's behalf cannot be ruled out. She restrained her thoughts and asked, "When did you come from Mumbai?" Sonika replied "last month". Lajwanti's thinking radars went active again "We're here for murder investigation," she continued, "..we suspect that the murders are connected to an unfortunate incident involving your brother few years ago and we believe someone in your family is involved in this murders..." Sonic's jaw tightened "What do you mean? What murders? My brother was missing much before my father died and I don't live here - how is our family a suspect?" Lajwanti replied in a calm tone "Your father is definitely dead but your brother is not known to be dead...so what is the proof that he is somehow not doing these murders!" Sonika's tone was even and without any trace of tension as she answered firmly, "In that case you prove that my brother is alive. Apart from me, I have one attendant in this house, search and see if you can find anyone else. If you find my brother, I will be the happiest to see him alive..." Lajwanti was a little surprised. She had not expected so much confidence however without showing any emotion she added "Of Course Ms Pradhan - local police will come tomorrow with a search warrant..I hope you will cooperate. We are taking our leave today, see you tomorrow..if your brother or you are involved in these murders in anyway, we will definitely find out." Lajwanti bit out the last line harshly. But Sonika Pradhan didn't flinch and said, "Sure madam - goodbye".

On their way out of the house, Lajwanti noticed Sonika's attendant leaving the house from the back porch and walking briskly across the edge of the hills towards the local market. She immediately ordered the car to follow the man keeping a safe distance. Sonika's overconfidence could not fool Lajwanti's experienced eyes. She was sure that Nandan was somewhere nearby only. They followed Bhusan till the time he crossed the immediate locality and headed towards the bazaar. They lost sight of the attendant once he entered an alley having throngs of shops. It was a very crowded area and it was not possible to continue in a car, so as per Lajwanti's instructions Sub-Inspector Naskar alighted from the car and walked towards the target shops. After sub-inspector Naskar returned, the car ran straight to the local police station. Whatever he found out by shadowing

Bhusan mandated local police reinforcement. Manpower would be needed to run the planned operation in the dark!

Lajwanti and her team were positioned near Sonika Pradhan's house for the last 45 minutes. The local police cordoned the area at some distance away. The clock showed it to be 8 o'clock in the evening.... However, it was almost night as hilly areas went to sleep early. Lajwanti's watchful eyes from her hideout spot regarded the almost uninhabited area carefully. today when Sub-Inspector Naskar had shadowed the attendant into the market, he had found him entering a Tours & Travels office. After Bhusan had left their premises Sub-Inspector Naskar had entered the office and interrogated the manager. He had learnt stuff which prompted Lajwanti not to delay for a second and be ready to make arrests before the bird flew the coup. The calculation was very simple. According to the Office record, Sonika had visited Kolkata a couple of times in their hired vehicles in the last one month. The dates were strangely coincident with the dates of murders in such a way that it was either one of two days prior to the incident dates that she reached Kolkata and always came back by the next day of the murders. Besides, according to the owner of the shop, the car was booked again at 9 pm today and this time for drop-off at the Bagdogra Airport. There was no room for doubt that the bird had planned to take off on the first flight of the morning. Lajwanti could have arrested Sonika straight away but she was waiting to see how Sonika's self-confidence would be shattered when they caught her in the act of fleeing! For some reason, albeit being a seasoned police officer devoid of general emotions, Lajwanti sought this piece of satisfaction.

When the clock struck quarter past nine, a bolero car stopped in front of the house. It stood there in silence as was the instructions given to the driver by Sonika's attendant. Five minutes after the car came to a stop, the grumpy attendant came out with two suitcases. Behind him Sonika Pradhan came out clad in a black long coat. At that moment, Sub-Inspector Naskar and Lajwanti jumped out of their hiding place behind a random high mound on the opposite side of the track and blocked the way of the car. Sonika and her attendant were shocked to see the armed police as the headlights of the car came on. The attendant immediately looked at his mistress's face as if waiting for an instruction - but Sonika was staring fixedly at Lajwanti, her face was bloodless and eyes were narrowed with despair. Aha! Lajwanti has been waiting for exactly this expression. She spoke in a firm voice "Don't try to run away...we have surrounded the area; you have been arrested for being directly involved in 4 murders that we are investigating..."

Sonika

Yes, I killed those bastards but not to avenge my brother – But myself ! Does that statement surprise you? You cannot digest the fact that I was Nandan

Pradhan before transitioning into Sonika Pradhan! Aha yes madam, I am Nandan, the very Nandan who was mercilessly raped by those beasts in the backyard garden of the school. The intoxicated insane bastards brutally injured me and raped me repeatedly! My screams were not heard over the noise of the music that was playing in the reunion party. When I was rescued the next morning I had been bleeding for over twelve hours. The doctor at the hospital told my father the truth about the nature of the assault, but my father was afraid of getting into trouble with the police. How would an uneducated low-paid school janitor fight with the "babus" of Kolkata? My helpless father tearfully told me "Beta forget all these incidents..." But I could not! ...you know for days and months I had nightmares of the same incident as if it was happening to me all over again and emotional trauma of the same was unbearable. I stopped eating...my fifteen year old innocent mind had died then. All my dreams of studying and growing up were vandalized madam. We were people of a small village from the hills and had no one to stand by us. My father could not stand my condition for long and one day he said "I will send you out of this place with whatever I have saved till date... you will not come back here again. You start a new life! I can't see you in this condition anymore...go away...looking at you makes me feel guilty that I could save you, my son." That day upon my father's advice I moved to Mumbai. The neighbors were told that I ran away. Thus started the fight of a young boy for a new life in

Mumbai. At this point of time even God took pity on me and I was taken into a NGO. The director was Sitara Devi ... a transgender social worker. I have not seen God, but I have felt the presence of God in Sitara Devi. Upon hearing my story, she accepted me like her own child. I was given proper education, thanks to her. During my stay with her one day I expressed my wish for transitioning. Sitara Devi initially did not agree at all but I kept telling her that I wanted a new life ... I wanted to erase my earlier identity from my mind and body alike. She finally gave in and consented and then after two long years of treatment and operation and hormone therapy, Nandan Pradhan was replaced by Sonika Pradhan. All these while I had kept in touch with my father, but he did not know about my transition. After my father died, I wanted to come back home once to pay my respect to the poor old man who had lost the battle with a broken heart. During my visit I stayed in a hotel and went to the school grounds before catching my return flight. Coincidentally there here was a parent teacher meeting that day and suddenly I saw one of those animals there... I think his son studied in the school.

Believe me, the moment I laid my eyes on that man, my whole body was paralyzed... the effort I had put in all these days to suppress the pain, resurfaced in an instant and I was consumed by an unquenching thirst for revenge. I felt these bastards had no right to live on. I knew I had to plan things carefully and locate the other 3 accomplices. I followed my target to

Kolkata and then spent almost 2 months searching social sites with the help of a freelance hacker. I knew by that time that one of the 4 was a NRI and he would be back in the city soon. The rest was very easy. My attendant Bhusan was a supari killer released on parole from jail. He was rehabilitating at the same NGO where I belonged and upon hearing my story, he agreed to kill once again, just to help me. He once used to kill for a living in exchange of money yet he was disgusted at what these filthy creatures had done to me only because I could not supply whores to their bed. It was not a difficult task for Bhusan to commit the murders without leaving any evidence, he was an expert in it. Luck was on my side, so I was able to enter their houses easily in my new avatar taking advantage of their lusty nature and no CC TV was installed in any of the localities. I have no remorse for my action...I know I took the law into my own hands...but those beasts deserved to die... I would have left the town long ago but I stayed on for a while with the desire to relive the memory of my father in my heart for the last time. I was surprised when the police came because I had not thought that anyone would find a connection of the murders to an incident that happened years ago. I was also sure of my new identity .. I thought no one would recognize Nandan. When I saw you, I knew that though you did not know the truth you were very near to finding the same out. I wanted to escape before you came back a second time...but..!

Lajwanti

Numerical murder case was solved by Police ... Newspapers were full of praises for Lajwanti and team. But Lajwanti requested to be transferred from the Homicide Department on immediate basis. She felt that it was her personal failure not to have caught the murderer alive and therefore she had no right to remain in Homicide Department. According to reports, the murderer Nandan Pradhan and his attendant escaped had escaped from the reach of the police that day and jumped off into a deep hilly cavern. Their bodies were not found and were expected lost somewhere in the ravine. The local police were of the belief that some mountain animal might have moved the bodies. DCP Lajwanti Lahiri took full responsibility of this incident and so did Sub-Inspector Naskar who also applied for transfer to the RAF Department of Kolkata Police. The case is about to be closed.

A couple of days after the incident

A young woman and a man boarded a flight from Bagdogra to Mumbai. The young woman did not take off her sunglasses during the entire flight. She was thinking quietly on her own that God comes to people in different forms, if one such form of that God was Sitaradevi and the other one was surely DCP Lajwanti Lahiri. Sonika was truly reborn now!

About the Authors

Riddhima Sen

Riddhima Sen is currently studying in Delhi Public School, Newtown, Kolkata IN class 12. She is an introvert who likes to read books and write poetry. She even likes to design garments and exciting apparels. She is a Social Media intern at Younity, a volunteer at Hamari Pahchan NGO, a Curriculum Writing intern at Team Everest, and the Vice President of the Architecture Club, SUPROS. She desires to enjoy life to the fullest and wants to try every activity under the sun. She likes to recite poems and compose lyrics as well. By participating in leadership programs, she has overcome her introversion to a great extent.

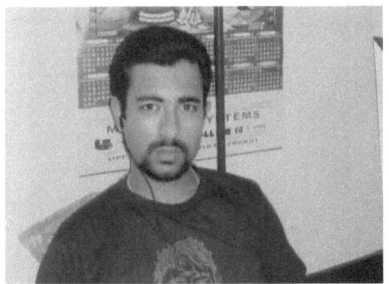

Chinmoy Nath

Chinmoy Nath, a Science graduate in Electronics and Telecommunications, took to composing short stories as a passion. He acted as a co-author in more than 20 anthologies. His solo collections of short stories, *Shouts of the Whispering Mind* and *The Mind Talks* were accepted well by readers. He was awarded as the Emerging author of the year 2022 by Ukiyoto Publishing and India's top 100 authors in India Prime Awards 2022 by Fox Clues. At present he is working on the sequel to his newly published novel *The Extraterrestrial Evolution*.

Mahendra Arya

Mahendra Arya is an engineer by qualification from Birla Institute Of Technology, Mesra. Mahendra writes in English as well as in Hindi. His writing spans across poetry, plays, fictions and religion. His published books include: *Beliefs of Arya Samaj* (a very useful guide book to understand Arya Samaj), *Facebook Friends* and *Tangents and a Circle* (both thrillers that keep the readers spellbound till the last page). His latest book *Kaikayi-The Misunderstood Queen* is a mythological fiction and has become very popular in 2022. *Facebook Friends* was awarded the Best Plot Of Year 2002 by Ukiyoto Publishing on September 18, 2022, in Delhi.

Juju's Pearls (Dr. Reemanshu Bansal)

Juju's Pearls (Dr. Reemanshu) is a blogger, writer, social worker, counselor, traveler and a Radiologist. Her first book *Momsie Popsie Diary—Tea Time Chitchat on Living Life* has thirteen literary awards, one Fellowship and three nominations to credit. It ranked on Amazon as #2. She has authored ten books (eight as co-authors). Her second book *My Mind's Café—28 Stories For a Love Tooth* has been launched in September 2022. She believes that helping others heal is a path to self healing.

Her blog – *reemanshu.blogspot.com*

Facebook Page: *Juju,s Reader Club*

Insta handle: *reemanshubansal*

Goodreads profile URL: *www.goodreads.com/reemanshu*

For any queries: *reemanshu2003@gmail.com*

Pabitra Adhikary

Pabitra Adhikary, an educator by profession, is the founder of Pabitra Sir Classes, a well known CAT GMAT preparation institute in Kolkata. Pabitra Adhikary is not only a dedicated faculty but also a passionate writer. He has written hundreds of poetries, stories, articles, science fiction, comics etc. His writings are stories about human relationship, adventure, nature and human relationship with nature, are available on Apple Books, Google Play Books, Amazon Audible, Storytel, Kobo, Audiobooks.com, Scribd etc. He also penned the *Adventures of Camelia* series, which were published periodically in Shuktara, a famous bengali monthly magazine in Kolkata.

Ashim Basnet

Ashim Basnet is a Hydro Power Engineer and a firm believer in sustainable development. An avid reader who has travelled the world through books, he is fascinated by the mountains and human behaviours, which are reflected in his writing. He simply loves the serene life up on the beautiful hills of Sikkim. He has a dream of one day going around the country and inspiring children to read, and to impart upon them the values and importance of education. This story is an endeavour of his to take a step towards that dream.

Revathi Raj Iyer

Revathi Raj Iyer is an author, editor, beta reader, book reviewer and Yoga/Fitness enthusiast. Professionally qualified in Law and as Company/Chartered Secretary from India and New Zealand, Revathi has worked in a multinational and also as Lecturer of Laws. After returning from Fiji, a spiritual enrichment break inspired her to write. Revathi has two titles to her credit: *My Friendship With Yoga* and *Syra's Secret— Diverse Short Stories From Siliguri, Singapore and Beyond*. Her next book *Tales from Sri Lanka and India* is under publication. Her stories, poems, book reviews and articles have been published both in print and online media. She enjoys writing short stories as she believes that fiction gives a chance to express and recreate life. She lives in the vibrant city of Ahmedabad with her husband and continues to write enchanting stories.

Harinder Cheema

Harinder Cheema is an internationally celebrated and versatile poet and author. She is the only Indian to receive the Naji Naaman International Literary Honor Prize for Complete Work in 2022. She shares space with other great world authors including the Birland Prime Minister. She is the author of two books: *The Temple Stop* and *Soul Chants, a Collection of Poetic Hymns*, published by Ukiyoto Publishing. She is the coauthor of 30 poetry anthologies and her articles have been published in various prestigious international magazines and coffee table books. She is also the proud recipient of many prestigious global awards and honours in the field of Literature.

Barnali Basu

Barnali is a self employed gynaecologist with a passion for writing, especially mystery and romance. She also plans to venture into horror and humor. Her favourite authors are Agatha Christie and Enid Blyton. She has won many creative writing contests and was on the editorial team for her college magazine. She has some short stories published in anthologies by different publications including Ukiyoto. She self-published a short mystery, *Two Worlds*, on Amazon Kindle. She lives in Guwahati with her husband and daughter.

Tulika Majumder

Tulika has been a successful corporate employee for almost 20 years. Always a bookworm and having a way with words, it was her dream to get her work published to the world. During the first phase of Covid lockdown, she published her first book *Saat Kando* with Asian Press Books. Her other published works include *Digantarekha*, *Machranga* and a compilation of Bengali horror stories called *Choturbhoy*; each having a significant dash of imagination, romance and thrills. A professional and a mother of a 15-year-old son, she is all set to make a mark in the minds of readers as a bilingual author. Her recent work in English is a full length binge novella titled *The Web Of Lies—a Regency Mystery*, published by Asian Press Books at the prestigious Press Club Of Kolkata amid eminent writing personalities!

www.ingramcontent.com/pod-product-compliance
Lightning Source LLC
LaVergne TN
LVHW041851070526
838199LV00045BB/1551